'Guy Adams is either barking mad or a genius, I haven't decided.' Mark Chadbourn

The author of the novels *The World House* and its sequel *Restoration*, Guy Adams gave up acting six years ago to become a full-time writer. This was silly, but thankfully he's kept busy, writing bestselling humour titles based on TV show *Life on Mars* and *Torchwood* novels *The House That Jack Built* and *The Men Who Sold The World*.

He has also written a pair of original Sherlock Holmes novels, *The Breath of God* and *The Army of Doctor Moreau*, as well as a biography of actor Leonard Rossiter and an updated version of Neil Gaiman's *Don't Panic: Douglas Adams & The Hitch-Hiker's Guide to the Galaxy*. He has also adapted three classic Hammer Horror movies, *Kronos*, *Hands of the Ripper* and *Countess Dracula*.

His website is: www.guyadamsauthor.com

Countess Dracula
GUY ADAMS

HAMMER

AN EXCLUSIVE MEDIA COMPANY

Published by Arrow Books in association with Hammer 2013

2 4 6 8 10 9 7 5 3 1

First published in Great Britain in 2013 by
Arrow Books in association with Hammer
Random House, 20 Vauxhall Bridge Road,
London SW1V 2SA

www.randomhouse.co.uk
www.hammerfilms.com

Addresses for companies within The Random House Group Limited can be
found at: www.randomhouse.co.uk/offices.htm

The Random House Group Limited Reg. No. 954009

A CIP catalogue record for this book
is available from the British Library

ISBN 9780099553861

The Random House Group Limited supports The Forest Stewardship
Council (FSC®), the leading international forest certification organisation.
Our books carrying the FSC label are printed on FSC® certified paper.
FSC is the only forest certification scheme endorsed by the leading
environmental organisations, including Greenpeace. Our paper
procurement policy can be found at:
www.randomhouse.co.uk/environment

MIX
Paper from
responsible sources
FSC® C016897

Typeset in Palatino by SX Composing DTP, Rayleigh, Essex
Printed and bound by CPI Group (UK) Ltd, Croydon, CR0 4YY

Foreword

On an early summer Saturday in 1970 I had a call from Alexander Paal, a fellow Hungarian, asking me to read that morning's *Times* as there was a well-researched article by another Hungarian on the life of Countess Elisabeth Bathory. I remembered the name from my school days; a powerful member of a great aristocratic family, who was famed for her cruelty. Once I read the piece it all came back: the gruesome story of a historical figure from the 16th century. According to the article, legend has it that Bathory hit a chambermaid so hard that blood from the girl's nose spurted onto her face. When Bathory washed the blood off and looked in the mirror her face appeared more beautiful and her skin whiter. She then began to bathe regularly in virgins' blood and is credited with the murder of over 600 peasant girls for cosmetic purposes.

I had arrived in London as a student following the Hungarian uprising in 1956, and promised myself I would not take on Hungarian subjects as a director in the UK. However, this was such a strong story I couldn't let it go. Having directed a number of costume dramas for BBC Television (*Wuthering Heights*, *The Tenant Of Wildfell Hall* and Henry James' *The Spoils Of Poynton*) I felt I'd done enough to prove that I could deal with non-Hungarian subjects. Especially since I had just directed my first Hammer feature film, *Taste The Blood Of Dracula*, which was very well received. The top critic of the day, the *Sunday Times*' Dilys Powell, called it 'a surprise from Hammer . . . pretty good; well played and directed with a straight face by a newcomer, Peter Sasdy: a nice feeling for the Victorian setting.'

Together with Alexander Paal I located the journalist behind the story and took an option on it during the same weekend. By Sunday evening we had a one-page outline for a film based on the life of Countess Elisabeth Bathory.

Following the success of *Taste The Blood Of Dracula* I was in favour because of the old principal that you're only as good as your last film and I still had my office in Hammer House on Wardour Street. It was decided that on Monday morning I would approach my big boss, Sir James Carreras, with our idea for my next film. It was about 11 o'clock when I got to see him. He read the page, asked a few questions about the way I saw the story developing, then looked at his watch and said: 'Come back at 12.45 with a coloured poster with a title on it. I'll take it with me to Genero's where I'm having lunch with the managing director of the Rank Organisation. Let's have another chat after lunch at about 3 o'clock. OK?'

We had our own graphics department on the top floor. I rushed up and explained Sir Jimmy's order, and while talking to the graphic artist about the story of the Countess and how she needed the continuous supply of blood – just like Dracula – the obvious choice for a title suddenly hit me: *Countess Dracula*!

At 12.45 the poster of a beautiful blonde, partially covered in blood with the title across her body, was on the desk of Sir James. After lunch I was summoned and with a huge smile on his face Sir James said: 'You'll start shooting *Countess Dracula* six weeks from today at Pinewood. I'll need a script in two weeks, a cast in three weeks – same budget as your last one with a 30 day schedule. OK?'

The rest is history. We started and finished the picture on time and I enjoyed the freedom Hammer gave me once they knew I'd deliver what they required. Hammer were always very good at choosing their subjects. Some thought audience identification with a 16th century blood-sucker might seem far-fetched, but in the 21st century women (and some men) spend thousands on modern cosmetics and face-lifts moti-vated by the same desire to look younger. At least they won't end up in a dungeon, as Countess Dracula did . . .

Peter Sasdy, Director
November 2012

PRE-CREDITS

ONSCREEN CAPTION: 12 August 1971

THE CAMERA PANS FROM THE TRAFFIC
WORKING ITS WAY ALONG HOLLYWOOD
BOULEVARD. WE FIND A SMALL PARKING
LOT, TWO OR THREE STORES AND AN
OPEN-TOPPED MINIBUS.

Hollywood eats. A fat beast of concrete, neon and
dust, jaws open, ever-hungry. And wherever a
behemoth eats, scavengers like Leo Hogarth
follow.

Stranded in the late sun of summer he broiled in
his black T-shirt and jeans, the official uniform of
The Golden Hollywood Tour, its logo screen-
printed across his chest like a rancher's branding
mark. As Leo was the managing director, guide
and creator of the tour he had only himself to
blame.

'Should have gone with white,' he moaned. 'But
black just looks classier.'

'You got that right,' said Roland, his African-American driver. 'I've been telling people that for years.'

Roland didn't live up to his own claim, rammed into a chauffeur's suit that was two sizes too small for him. 'Quit your moaning,' Leo had told him when he'd found it at a closing-down party store. 'People only see you from the waist up.' Which was true, and a reason to be thankful, because Roland had to keep the trousers unfastened in order to still breathe while manoeuvring the open-top bus around Hollywood Hills.

'At least people can't see the sweat patches,' Roland added. 'In white, you'd look like a Holstein by noon.'

'I wouldn't care so much if we were getting the numbers in,' said Leo, looking around the corner at the short queue that was beginning to form for the three-o'clock tour. 'I mean, look at it: I'd make more money cleaning buses than driving around in them.'

'It's a quiet year,' said Roland, lighting a stubby joint and settling back into his usual attitude of casual apathy. 'There's a recession.'

'There's always a fucking recession.'

The queue was only five people long: two fat couples and an old guy. 'They're not even a good audience,' sighed Leo, reaching over and taking a drag on the joint. 'One of 'em looks like he'll be lucky to last the trip.'

'As long as he pays he can die whenever he likes.'

'Yeah, senior rate. That's two bucks blown before I even leave the kerb.'

'Better than nothing.'

'Says you. I pay you a wage – what do you care if I lose my shirt?'

Roland shrugged. He knew better than to get into an argument. Leo was blowing off steam: it didn't mean a thing.

'Wait a minute.' Leo perked up suddenly. 'All is not lost!'

A pair of girls were ambling over to the queue. Both of them were blonde and were wearing bikini tops and denim shorts, the uniform of the college student on holiday.

'You may be poor but your dick still works.' Roland found this incredibly funny but that was just an effect of the dope.

'Let's get over there before they change their minds.'

Leo checked his reflection quickly in a shop window, just to make sure his T-shirt was tucked in.

'Black is class,' Roland assured him, pinching out his joint and slipping it into his shirt pocket for later.

'Good afternoon, everybody!' Leo announced, arms spread Christ-wide, ever the showman when he was on display.

Roland hung back as always, waiting for the audience's attention to be fully on Leo so that he could sneak into the driver's seat without them seeing the top of his trousers gaping open.

'Thank you for joining us here on The Golden Hollywood Tour,' Leo said, 'where we bring the history of Tinseltown to life before your very eyes! Every star, every story, every scandal – all from the comfort of our open-topped tour vehicle.'

'Must be a long tour,' the old guy mumbled. But Leo chose to ignore the implied criticism; the oldster was far from the first customer to make the comment.

'You'll certainly get your money's worth,' he replied, deciding to stick to the subject and sell the small group their tickets before anyone changed their mind.

As they filed onto the bus, Leo tried hard to fix things so that the girls would sit up front with him. For the life of him he couldn't distinguish between them, so typical of their type was each one.

'My name's Brandi!' announced one of them. 'And this is my friend Cheryl.'

'We're here for five days!' announced Cheryl, though Leo hadn't asked how long they were staying. 'Brandi's dad paid for it because he thinks she's going to be a star.'

Leo could think of only one branch of the movie industry in which they would excel. 'That's just great,' he said. 'The dream starts right here, huh?'

'Yeah,' said Brandi, only too happy to believe him. 'We're going to see my future house!'

'*Our* future house,' Cheryl laughed. 'Wherever you go you'll need your manager with you.'

'Yeah,' chirped Brandi again. But the sentiment didn't reach her eyes. She held up a fat paperback book. Leo looked at the title: *The Hit List: 1000 Stars of Hollywood.* 'I'm going to be in this one day,' she said, and hugged it to her like a child with a teddy bear.

'Believe it,' Leo replied – unnecessarily, because she so clearly did.

He sat them down on the seat next to him before reminding himself to pay attention to the rest of the party.

The first of the two couples looked like they had come on holiday by mistake. The wife's expression was one of sour disapproval as she glanced cautiously at her seat before sitting down on it. She gazed at Leo with clear scepticism. Her husband simply stared out at the road, a thick white line of sunblock painted down his nose like tribal warpaint.

'I always think it's nice if we each introduce ourselves,' said Leo, looking towards them. 'My name's Leo and, as well as being your guide today, I'm the author of the best-selling book *Hollywood Glitter*.' It was certainly the best-selling book to be offered on the tour and that was enough for him. 'At the end of the tour you'll have an opportunity to buy a signed copy as a souvenir.' He looked at the disapproving wife. 'Would you like to tell us all who you are?'

'Doesn't seem like I have much choice,' she replied, glancing around in obvious displeasure. 'My name's Margaret Riggers and this is my husband Tony. We're visiting from Colorado where my husband runs an extremely successful car-hire agency.'

'All the way from the mountains!' laughed Leo. 'Glad you're with us.' He looked at the next couple, a diminutive pair dressed in outfits that seemed to be colour-coded, a vision in taupe and cream.

'My name's Jerry,' the husband announced in a cheerful Southern accent, 'and this is my wife Vonda. We actually won our trip here on an episode of *Celebrity Shuffle*!'

Vonda couldn't have been more proud of him for having brought up the subject. 'We beat Al Lewis with a pair of queens!'

Leo could have done without the mental picture this conjured. 'You card sharks, you! Remind me not to get in a game while we're on our travels.'

'We'd have the shirt off your back!' Jerry promised.

Leo was pleased to notice this made Cheryl giggle. 'In this heat I just might let you!' He looked at the elderly man who had placed himself right at the back, head down as if embarrassed even to be on board. 'And you are?'

'Eager to get going,' came the quiet reply. The old man looked up and Leo was struck by the colour of his eyes: they were the palest, most striking blue he had ever seen. Although he might have aged, this guy had once been a player in his day, that was for sure.

Once it was clear that nobody was going to ignore him, the old man sighed. 'Gary Holdaway.'

'Pleasure to have you with us, Mr Holdaway,' said Leo. 'Well, then,' he said, 'all that remains is for me to introduce your driver, Roland Johns –' Roland gave a casual wave from his seat. '– and we'll be on our way.'

Roland pulled out into the traffic, relying on the philosophy of bus drivers everywhere: 'Nobody wants to screw with you when you're this damn big.' The manoeuvre made Margaret Riggers gasp but they got into a lane without colliding with anything. Leo launched into his script, a warmed-over rehash of Kenneth Anger's *Hollywood Babylon* with a few extra invented tales thrown in. Nobody cared about facts, they just wanted gossip.

'What does "prodigious" mean?' Cheryl asked him when he alluded to the legendary manhood of Errol Flynn. Leo would have showed her if only he could.

They headed up into the hills, with Leo pointing out one-time homes of the barely remembered in this most forgetful of industries.

'Of course,' he said, filling a gap in the procession of sights, 'it's worth remembering that Hollywood was built out of nothing. The first studios only came out here because they were avoiding the legal minefield created by Thomas Edison who sued anyone he considered was illegally using the technology that he had invented.

'All of this was nothing but dirt and farms, wide-open spaces waiting for the movies to come and make their mark on them. In 1900 it was a small town – a hotel, a main street and a boxcar line into Los Angeles. A two-hour journey through the vineyards and orchards. But Hollywood builds its legends quickly. It grew and grew until Los Angeles and it met, the larger city swallowing the smaller and making the place its own.

'The most iconic presence of all, the Hollywood sign, was originally built to advertise a chunk of real estate. *Hollywood Land*. The name came from something overheard on a train journey, describing someone's Florida holiday home.

'Legends. Born quickly, built in a frenzy and then left to bloom. Much like the legends that sur-rounded the actors that would earn their fame here. Some of the performers came from the theatre, many were no more than hopefuls, faces that fit.

Flooding in from all corners of the globe, the studios would take them and embellish them, give them their legend. Let them soar.'

'Stop the bus!' shouted Holdaway, moving with a speed that was clearly beyond his age, swaying at the rail as he stood up and looked beyond the road.

Roland, out of panic, did just that. He swerved to the shoulder, a roar of car horns washing over them as the vehicle screeched to a halt.

All the passengers fell forward and Leo tumbled onto his back in the centre aisle. There was an amplified curse, then a whine of feedback as the microphone left his hand and collided with the speaker.

'What the fuck?' he shouted, more at Roland than at the old man who had fallen against the back of the seat in front and got himself wedged between the two.

'There's no need for that!' insisted Margaret Riggers, though whether she meant Leo's language or the emergency stop nobody could be sure.

'I thought there was something wrong,' said Roland, looking around in confusion and embar - rassment. 'Did I hit something?'

Nobody bothered to answer him, all of them too concerned with themselves. Vonda had let go of her capacious purse and was shuffling around on her hands and knees trying to gather up her belong- ings. Crushed tissues like sickly roses, mascara stick, loose change, hairbrush and confectionery wrappers, all hoovered back into place before anyone else could comment on them.

'I think I have whiplash,' Margaret Riggers was insisting. 'You'd better hope you have good insurance cover, Mr Hollywood, or you'll be in hock to me for the rest of your life.'

Leo chose to ignore the threat for now, his attention on the old man who was pulling himself upright and looking out across the road.

'Why did you shout?' Leo asked him. 'What was the problem?'

'Her house,' Holdaway insisted. 'You were going right past her house.'

'Whose house?'

Leo rubbed the back of his head where he was pretty sure a bruise was building that would be big enough to need a hat of its own. He walked over to Holdaway who was still staring off between the palm trees.

'Elizabeth,' the old man said, his tone wistful, as if he was discussing someone lost.

'Elizabeth?'

Holdaway looked at Leo and those beautiful eyes had disbelief in them. 'You must remember her – she lived just there.'

Leo swallowed a little ball of panic. He hated being caught out in his lack of knowledge, it was the sort of thing that lost an audience in a heartbeat.

Of course, he wasn't an expert: the history of this mad town was just too sprawling and the family tree of stardom spread its branches wide. He played for time.

'There are a lot of Elizabeths,' he said, though his mental count was still coming up short. 'Elizabeth who?'

Holdaway's disbelief turned into sadness. 'Legends soar, isn't that what you said?' He looked away again and Leo stared in the same direction. Beyond the trees he saw a road cutting further up through the hills before sinking away into a valley. The barest glint of sun on glass caught his eye. There was certainly some kind of residence up there, though it didn't belong to anyone he knew from his scant research.

'They crash all too easily, too,' continued Holdaway. 'Elizabeth Sasdy. Once a queen of this town, adored by all. Now you don't even remember her.'

Leo didn't, but he wasn't going to admit it easily. 'Elizabeth Sasdy? She lived up there?'

There was a rustle of paper from behind him as Brandi worked her way through her book.

'Elizabeth Sasdy,' she said, stumbling slightly over the surname. 'Born Nadasdy, Hungary, 1885. Silent-movie actress . . .' She looked up in confusion. 'Silent? She never said anything?'

'It means the movies were silent,' said Leo with a

sigh, though in truth he was glad to have the opportunity to talk from a position of knowledge. 'All movies were silent – or mostly silent – until the late 1920s.'

Brandi laughed. 'They can't have been much good, then! I knew that they didn't have colour all those years ago but who knew they couldn't even speak either?'

Cheryl laughed along with her.

'Some of the all-time classics of cinema were silent,' said Leo, 'Griffith's *Birth of a Nation* . . .'

'Tedious,' said Holdaway, his attention back with them. 'Not a patch on Elizabeth's greatest works.'

'You're obviously quite a fan,' said Leo. He smiled, hoping that he could get the old man onside through a little flattery.

'I was, but not just that. I worked with her . . .'

Leo's mood picked up – it just might be that this trip could be turned around after all. 'You worked with her?'

'On a couple of pictures.' Holdaway looked over at Brandi and Cheryl. 'Though you sure won't find me in that book of yours. My career never really took off. Not like hers.'

Leo made a snap decision. 'You want we should go take a look at the old place?' he suggested. 'You could maybe even relive a few memories for us.'

Holdaway looked at him for a moment and then

smiled. 'You like the idea of a guest star, huh?' he asked. Then he nodded. 'What the hell. I'll tell you what I remember but I can't promise you'll like all of it. Elizabeth was . . . well, she had a reputation. They called her the Countess, because of her accent, but the things she got up to in that place . . .'

Leo didn't need to hear more. He knew what his audiences liked, the sleazier the better. 'Roland, get over there.' He held out his arm to Holdaway. 'You maybe want to sit up front so you can tell him the way?'

'Does this mean we're going to skip Kirk Douglas's place?' moaned Vonda. 'I really wanted to see him.'

'Just a little detour,' said Leo. 'A special bonus, some first-hand Hollywood history.'

'I can manage,' Holdaway insisted, pushing past Leo and settling down next to Roland.

'I'll have to go on a little way,' the driver explained, 'and switch direction at the bridge.'

'Probably making it up as he goes along,' said Margaret Riggers. 'I don't believe a word of it.'

Maybe not, thought Leo, but at least it's shut you up about litigation.

It took them five minutes to change direction but then they were off the main strip and heading into the hills. It occurred to Leo that the old house was bound to have new occupants and he hoped there was somewhere they could park and get a good view without having to deal with overeager security personnel.

He needn't have worried. Once they had climbed a short distance Holdaway directed Roland down into the valley and soon the house was ahead of them. If it had any new occupants they hadn't yet made their presence felt. As Leo and his group descended towards the building they had an aerial view of the place and the closer they got the more its run-down state became clear.

It had been built in the Spanish style but its white walls had turned smoker's-teeth yellow and its orange tiles were cracked and thick with moss. The central courtyard, which had once been laid out to perfection, was now no more than a chaos of bougainvillea, palm leaves and oleander. A driveway, openly accessible because the pair of wrought-iron gates that should have given it privacy had swung wide and rusted in place, was a minefield of potholes and weeds, grass bursting forth in sun-dried clumps all the way along it to the front door.

'Oh, Elizabeth,' said Holdaway, looking at the place, 'your castle has fallen.'

'The place is a dump,' agreed Jerry, with an enthusiastic chuckle. 'I wonder how much they want for it?'

'You reckon we could take a peek?' asked Vonda. 'I don't see that it's trespassing, not with the gates open like that.'

Leo might have pointed out that just because someone left their door open didn't mean that the law considered it fine to walk right in. But, looking at his passengers, he saw so much excited curiosity that he couldn't help but pander to it. 'Why not?' he said. 'After all, if Gary here was a friend . . .'

'I was never that,' said Holdaway, sitting back down. 'Nobody was. But there's no one here anyway, so who's to tell?'

'Let's just get on with it,' said Tony Riggers and Leo realised this was the first time he'd heard the man speak. It seemed to surprise his wife slightly, too. She glanced at him, perhaps remembering what his voice sounded like after all these years. 'I want to be back in town on the outside of a cool Margarita, and the sooner we get this over with the sooner I'll have salt on my lips.'

Roland looked at Leo, who nodded. Grinning, he selected first gear and took the bus slowly down the drive. Margaret was moaning again immediately the suspension took its first jolt as it navigated the potholes.

Leo looked to either side of the drive, seeing the thick grass choked with weeds, and wondered how somewhere like this could have been allowed to deteriorate so far. Surely a chunk of real estate like this should have been worth a fortune? He was as eager to hear about it from the old man as were the rest of his passengers: what had happened here that had marked the place out as a ruin?

Roland gave up two-thirds of the way towards the house, deciding that if they risked going along the driveway any further they might never get the bus back out again. 'What say you all walk from here?' he suggested. 'I'll turn the bus around.'

'We have to walk?' moaned Vonda, 'I didn't bring the right shoes.'

'Maybe just take a quick look around,' said Leo. 'Shame not to explore after all – the home of a genuine star!'

'Maybe you'll buy this place!' Cheryl joked with Brandi. 'We could put in a pool.'

'There used to be one,' said Holdaway. 'It's probably full of toads now.'

They walked up to the front door, all of them staring at it for a moment before Tony Riggers took the bull by the horns. 'Christ's sake,' he muttered, shoving at it with his shoulder.

The door swung open and its rusted hinges snapped. He was left holding it in his hands.

'I think we can safely say that nobody's been here for a few years,' he said, leaning the detached door against the front wall. 'So nobody's likely to be coming along soon, either.'

'Then what are we waiting for?' asked Brandi. She and Cheryl laughed and ran inside the house.

Their voices echoed off the high ceiling of a

massive entrance hall, a cylindrical room with a large stairway at the far end. The strange sense of abandonment continued inside. A Turkish rug took up the centre of the tiled floor, its colour faded, its weave frayed. It had an animal scent to it and Leo scowled. Clearly, local beasts had made the place their own and he hoped they weren't going to come face to face with a pack of feral dogs in the dining hall.

Holdaway headed straight through, ignoring the staircase and moving deeper inside the house. 'I want to see the courtyard,' he said. 'The garden . . . that was where she really lived. All of this was just the walls that kept everyone else out.'

'Not working so well now, are they?' said Margaret Riggers, strolling past him, acting as if she owned the place.

'No secrets here any more,' Holdaway said as they came out in a large living area. 'Nothing left to hide.'

There was a big central fireplace, now little more than a pile of wet claylike soot. To one side there was a seating area, with chairs still in place, their upholstery torn or absent altogether, their flanks scratched and gouged by animals that had made beds of them. On the other side was a large dining table, made from a heavy dark wood that had survived the years of neglect better than anything else they had seen so far.

'What I wouldn't give to take that back home,' said Jerry. 'I could bring that up so you could see your goddamn face in it.'

'Well,' said Margaret, 'if that wouldn't be enough to put you off your meal I don't know what would.'

'Are you calling my husband ugly?' Vonda asked. But Margaret ignored her, heading straight over to the far side where there would once have been a massive set of French windows but which was now open to the air. Beyond, sunk down so that they loomed over it, they could see the massive courtyard garden, a space all of five hundred feet long and three hundred wide. It was like looking down into a small jungle and as Leo came up behind Margaret and Holdaway he couldn't help but imagine what might be inside it.

'There's probably animals in there,' he said, which made Holdaway laugh.

'There certainly always were,' the old man said. 'Dangerous animals indeed.' He turned to address them all with a slight theatricality that Leo couldn't fail to notice. Once an actor, always an actor . . .

'The silver screen was where Elizabeth Sasdy's reputation was born, that courtyard was where it grew and, eventually, that was where it also died. In blood, death and terror.'

'Sounds groovy,' said Cheryl, laughing. 'Tell us more.'

And so he did.

FIRST REEL: THE THIEVING MAGPIE

THE SCREEN SPUTTERS WITH PRINT DAMAGE, SCRATCHES AND LIGHT FLASHES. AN OLD NEWSREEL BEGINS TO PLAY. SEPIA-TONED, OVER-CRANKED SO THE FOOTAGE MOVES AT ONE AND A HALF TIMES NATURAL SPEED. CROWDS OF PEOPLE GATHER AROUND GRAUMAN'S CHINESE THEATRE. A TANGIBLE SENSE OF EXCITEMENT.

VOICE-OVER: And here we are at the Chinese Theatre on Hollywood Boulevard where crowds gather to wait for the thrilling premiere of the new picture from Sunset Studios, *Where the Devil Takes Me*. A savage romance set against the backdrop of Eastern Mongolia, it promises to be a smash hit with the public and critics alike.

A LIMOUSINE PULLING UP AGAINST THE KERB, THE CROWDS JUMPING.

V.O. (Cont.) And we all know why! Here they are, Hollywood's golden couple and stars of *Where the Devil Takes Me* – Elizabeth Sasdy and Frank Nayland!

THE COUPLE GET OUT OF THE CAR, SMILING GRACIOUSLY TO THEIR FANS. SASDY IS BLONDE, PERHAPS A LITTLE MORE CURVACEOUS THAN IS THE CURRENT PETITE FASHION. SHE IS WEARING A WHITE GOWN THAT SHIMMERS DESPITE THE DAMAGED FILM FOOTAGE. NAYLAND IS EVERY INCH THE MALE IDOL, SQUARE-JAWED, SLICKED-BACK HAIR AND A PHYSIQUE THAT FILLS OUT EVERY CORNER OF HIS IMMACULATE TUXEDO.

V.O. (Cont.) Who doesn't love these stars of our age? Whose hearts couldn't be warmed by their story?

CLOSE-UP ON SASDY AS SHE LAUGHS, HER EYES LUMINESCENT.

V.O. (Cont.) Elizabeth Sasdy, the all-American farm girl from Wisconsin. Spotted by a

Hollywood talent scout, she has shot to fame over the last three years, appearing in over ten films for Sunset. Living the dream, proof that anybody can make it in this country of ours!

CLOSE-UP ON NAYLAND, WAVING AT THE CROWD. HE APPEARS TO SPOT A FACE HE KNOWS. HE POINTS AND SMILES.

V.O. (Cont.) Frank Nayland, lord of the English stage, now idol of the silver screen, the man all the ladies wanted to walk them up the aisle.

TWO-SHOT. NAYLAND AND SASDY PULLING CLOSE TOGETHER, SHE LOOKING UP AT HIM WITH CLEAR ADORATION IN HER EYES, HE LOOKING DOWN AT THE MOST PRECIOUS THING IN HIS WORLD.

V.O. (Cont.) But plucky Elizabeth beat them all to it! The happiest couple in the country, Frank Nayland and Elizabeth Sasdy – it's not just the moving pictures that have happy endings!

NEWSREEL FLICKERS. THE FILM RUNS OUT, LEAVING THE SCREEN A BURNING WHITE.

FADE TO BLACK

It took Frank Nayland a few moments to discern what it was that he was seeing, to translate the multitude of limbs, the writhing of sweating flesh and break it down into its constituent parts.

'What?' his wife asked, raising her mouth from the groin of the Puerto Rican boy splayed under her. 'You don't think to knock?'

What with her thick Hungarian accent and her slavering lips Nayland had trouble understanding her words, though her meaning was clear enough. She hated nothing more than being interrupted. Her other attendant clearly had no such compunction, manoeuvring in behind her and pounding away at her rump with the sort of relish that can only come from a young man who earns his living by the hour.

Elizabeth continued to stare at Nayland, seemingly unmoved by the exertions behind her.

'Get out,' she said, her voice quiet and flat. 'The last thing I need to see is your pathetic face.' She protected herself from seeing more of it by closing her eyes and resuming her suckling.

Nayland left the room, saying nothing.

He stood in the hallway for a moment, staring up at the Lempicka portrait of his treacherous wife and wishing he could take a knife to it, maybe carve the smile he couldn't find on his own face into the oil-paint representation of hers.

As the noise of sex built to a crescendo behind him he decided to at least save himself the experience of hearing every pump and thrust. He made his way down their wide staircase, looking down at the perfection of their entrance hall, the opulent foyer that greeted all who came to their door. If only it matched their actual life.

'I didn't see you go up there,' said Patience, their housekeeper, 'or I would have told you not to.' Her face was as impassive as ever, always the figure of propriety even here in a house of sin.

'Doesn't matter,' Nayland said. 'I should know better by now.'

Patience nodded slightly, though whether in agreement or deference he couldn't decide. He didn't care to guess so he walked off, making his way out into the garden.

The air was cool and it felt like just what he needed. He sat on the steps and let it chill some of the anger from his face. That emotion was quickly followed by embarrassment. After all, he had never been in any doubt concerning the nature of their marriage. They were a Hollywood confection, all part of the Sasdy Legend, like Elizabeth's Wisconsin homeland. He was window dressing, beefcake to help sell the story of her pure romantic heart. If she even had a heart – he had yet to glimpse it.

Not that Nayland hadn't benefited from the arrangement, of course. Attached to hers, his reputation had risen just as high, his fortunes swollen as large. It had been a sensible business arrangement and one that he had entered into willingly, because at the time he hadn't had the slightest feeling for Elizabeth. It was a constant source of self-disgust that now, after years of abuse and infidelity, he had fallen in love with her. What sort of idiot did that make him?

There was the distant sound of birds in the trees and Nayland looked towards the hills, watching as something took to the sky and soared towards the horizon. He envied it.

The doorbell rang and he got to his feet, the false smile he dropped into place on his face brilliant through years of practice.

He heard Patience open the door. That sound was followed by the garrulous voice of Fabio, their manager. The last person he wanted to see.

Fabio wore his ethnicity like a badge, claiming to have Sicilian blood and the ear of every unsavoury crime lord in the country. Nayland didn't believe a word of it. Fabio was corrupt enough, of course – he worked in Hollywood – but Nayland didn't believe a real criminal would have the patience needed to deal with him. Five minutes, Nayland thought, that's all it would take in the company of genuine mobsters before someone reached for a gun and put everyone out of their misery.

'Hey, Frankie!' Fabio shouted, holding out his short arms. To Nayland he looked like a beetle trapped on its back in the sun, his massive belly the greater part of him. Nayland accepted the hug. The manager buried his face into the actor's chest like a frightened child seeking comfort.

'So glad I caught you on your own first,' he said in a stage whisper. 'Where is she?'

'Busy.'

'Then we can talk?'

Nayland nodded and led him back out to the garden. On the way, Fabio ordered something to drink from Patience as if she was his servant, not Nayland's.

They sat at a small table by the pool, Nayland trying to soak up the calm around him and cancel out Fabio's whine.

'Chester's been calling again,' he was saying. 'He really wants you for the picture and it's perfect for you. You play a policeman in a little town . . . I don't know where the hell it's supposed to be . . . Bavaria, fucking Transylvania . . . you know, whatever set's still standing at Universal. Horse-drawn carts and old guys with their pants tucked into their socks. Something's draining blood from the local maidens and it's your job to hunt them down.'

'Sounds great,' Nayland replied with heavy sarcasm.

'Hey, it's work and the audiences love this shit. They'll get in Lugosi or Atwill or Karloff or one of those guys and they'll be screaming in the aisles. That's what the people want these days, you know? Mad scientists and vampires.'

'I don't like that kind of picture.'

'Who cares? I'm not asking you to watch the fucking thing, I'm asking you to be in it. Take the cheque, damn you – they're few and far between these days.'

'What happened to all the romantic leads?'

'They went to the younger and brighter guys. Come on, Frankie, you know this – don't make me go through it with you.'

'I'm not old.'

'In Hollywood terms you are, Frankie. Besides, you know it's not just about your age. Your name isn't what it once was.'

'Because of Elizabeth.'

'Because of Elizabeth, and if you insist on staying here . . .'

'You're the one that said we should be married in the first place.'

'That was then. Years ago. Aeons. Whole genera-tions have passed. Back then it was the thing to do, then she began having her . . . problems.' Brutal as Fabio could be, he knew better than to be too blunt in front of Nayland. 'At which point she became poison. You should have been out of this marriage

26

three years ago. Nobody would have cared. If you'd done that . . .'

'I'd still have a career?'

'Oh hell, Frankie, you still have a career now if you want it. But you're not making it easy for me, you know? You're being obstructive, being . . .'

'Faithful?'

'Don't give me that!' Fabio seemed genuinely angry now, leaning back in his chair and fixing his client with a puffy-faced stare. 'You're supposed to be an actor, damn it, so learn when to maintain character and when not. Back then it made sense for the two of you to get together. Christ, it's tried and tested . . . the people love a romantic story. You gave her legitimacy, she gave you a profile. You had a couple of years of box-office gold. But then . . .'

'Everything changed.'

'What doesn't, Frankie? Life is one big change and you have to ride it. Elizabeth was great when all she had to do was make love to the camera. But you know as well as I do that it's hard to maintain the pretence of a poor girl made good from Connecticut . . .'

'Wisconsin.'

'Wherever. The point is, audiences liked that story, they bought into it. What are they going to think when this all-American beauty opens her mouth and they can't understand a word she says?'

'Her accent's not that strong.'

'Frankie, she sounds like she's chewing the words up and spitting them out. Nobody cares with the likes of Lugosi, they love it, they make him even more horrible . . . but Elizabeth? Who wants to fall in love with someone who sounds like she milks yaks for her morning coffee?'

Nayland might have admitted that he had.

'She's taking lessons.'

'I know, with Cecil Lundy. He's good. Hell, he's the best. But he tells me it's like trying to push soup uphill. She ain't going to be Fay Wray any time soon. Besides . . .' Fabio sighed and lowered his voice. 'I hate to say this, you know I do, but she's losing her looks, she's getting old. If she still had the magic she had ten years ago, then, screw it, I could have sold her into anything, whatever she sounds like. But now?

'Hollywood is a heartless bitch, Frankie: it doesn't give two fucks about your feelings. Elizabeth has had her day. Short of a miracle she's not going to be working again soon and unless you jump ship she's going to end up taking you down with her.'

Elizabeth lay back in her bed and let the breeze of the fan dry the sweat of sex from her. Just for a moment, the briefest of seconds, she was happy.

It never lasted.

'I don't pay you to sleep,' she told the Puerto

Rican, pushing him with her foot. He sat up, bleary-eyed. What was he on? He was nineteen or twenty but his pretty face was hanging from the bones in a way that spoke of strong dope.

'You want go again?' he asked, showing some of the stamina of his age. A listless hand grabbed at her thigh.

'No, I want you gone. Both of you.'

She slapped at her other paid lover, an Eastern European who had tanned his skin to a perfect bronze that must have taken almost constant effort to maintain. He was a beautiful little bastard, she thought, and he knew it.

They slid off the bed and Elizabeth sighed as she watched them shuffling around the room in search of their clothes. Two perfect statues. The Puerto Rican sneaked a quick glance in the mirror, check-ing himself out. And why not? She remembered a time when the mirror had been a good friend to her rather than an embarrassing relative she tried to avoid. She avoided it now as she got up and moved over to her dressing table, picking up an envelope of cash and flinging it to the Eastern European. He made to open the envelope and check its contents but then thought better of it. There's a little brain in there, she decided: he knew well enough not to risk angering her by implying that he didn't trust her.

In silence they filed out, the Puerto Rican offering a half-hearted wave as he left the room.

Alone, Elizabeth gave it a couple of minutes and then got up. She took a cigarette from a box on the dresser and stood smoking it in front of the mirror. She analysed what she saw: her whole body appeared to hang an inch or so lower than it should have. She experimented by cupping her breasts higher and pulling the loose skin over her belly towards her hips so that her abdomen was taut again. But sooner or later you had to let go. She turned to her side, scowling at her ever-increasing buttocks, pouring themselves across the back of her cellulite-pocked thighs. It was as though her perfect body was becoming hidden inside an ill-fitting bag of skin and fat.

Her face was the worst: deep lines around her eyes and lips, the constantly reappearing grey roots in her hairline, the puffy bags beneath her eyes. Her face showed every year and more – she had lived hard here in America and, for all the effort that had gone into hiding that fact from the general public, her skin knew.

Elizabeth stubbed the cigarette out against her reflection and went to the window. She could hear the voices of Fabio and Nayland filtering up from the garden so she opened the window and leaned out, trying to hear what they were discussing. It took no time at all for her to wish she couldn't. It seemed that she was fated to have her fading powers pointed out to her from all sides.

She felt the increasingly frequent sensation of

panic building up in her chest and had to sit down on the bed before she fell over. Usually the tremors faded quickly but this time her whole body felt as if it had tensed, her lungs short of air, her heart beating away like a studio fanfare.

She struggled to her feet and ran into the en-suite bathroom, convinced she was having a heart attack, quite sure that she was going to collapse at any moment. Catching sight of her panicked face in the bathroom mirror, all gritted teeth and red, blotchy skin, she might almost have wished it. Almost. She opened the bathroom cabinet and hunted through the pills, sending bottles flying as she found her downers. She popped the lid and took two, sitting down on the lid of the toilet to try and get her breathing back under control. Eventually the panic subsided, leaving her feeling drained and spent – and every single one of her forty-four years.

Nayland was doing his best to let Fabio's words bounce off him like droplets of rain. If he sheltered from their impact they couldn't soak him and chill his bones.

'I think it's best if we stop talking about this,' he said, 'I'm not leaving Elizabeth and so the conver - sation's pointless.'

Fabio sighed and shook his head. 'God knows what she's done to inspire such loyalty. Any wife of mine acted like she did . . .'

'But she's not your wife,' Nayland said, digging his nails into the surface of the table. 'So just drop the subject.'

Fabio held up his hands in surrender. 'Fine, fine . . . So, what about the horror picture? Can I tell Chester you'll see him?'

Nayland started to shake his head. 'It's not my kind of movie.'

'It's the only kind of movie you're getting offered,' Fabio shouted, finally losing his temper all the way. 'What the hell point is there in my representing you if you don't ever take a goddamn job? Nothing lasts for ever, Frank, not even money. You've got to start working again or soon there'll be nothing left for any of us.' He leaned over. 'And what do you think the "Countess" upstairs will do then, huh? You think she's going to hang around once the cash has dried up?'

'All right,' Nayland said. 'I'll see Chester.'

Fabio was instantly all smiles again, 'There we go – finally he sees sense. Money in the bank and my boy's face back up on the screen where it belongs. You won't regret it. Chester makes good movies, it'll be great. This is a whole new audience for you.'

'A screaming one.'

'Screams, laughter, tears . . . who cares as long as they're making a fucking noise, right?'

'You always were in tune with the art of this business.'

'Art? I tell you what art I like, Frankie boy: pictures of dead presidents. Those portraits are food for the soul.'

Elizabeth appeared at the top of the steps leading down to the pool. She was still dressed only in her silk robe, her hair vaguely brushed. She wouldn't dream of making an effort for Fabio – he wasn't important enough to her – though she kissed both his cheeks with such enthusiasm that a casual observer might have thought otherwise.

'Darling Fabio,' she said. Was she trying to mask her accent a little? Nayland thought she was. 'How lovely to see you, as always.'

'And you, sweetie,' he replied, 'and as beautiful as ever.'

She gave him a scathing look which he had the common sense to ignore.

'So what brings you here?' she asked. 'Countless offers of work, no doubt?'

'A movie role for Frankie, yeah,' Fabio replied. 'A great opportunity to bring him in front of a whole new audience.'

'It's a horror picture,' Nayland muttered.

Elizabeth wrinkled her nose. 'I can't abide them.'

'Thankfully the great American public doesn't agree with you. It's all they want these days,' Fabio retorted.

'And nothing for me?' she asked, knowing the answer but wanting to goad him.

'I thought we agreed that we would hold off on staging your comeback until you'd completed your sessions with Lundy?'

'Oh, but I grow impatient.'

'Timing is everything, dear heart – unless you would be happy to let the studio redub your voice?'

'Any director who tried that with me . . .' She smiled. 'Well, I doubt I'd ever talk to him again.'

Nayland could see that Fabio was considering making a joke of that but thankfully the manager decided against it at the last moment. Instead he just shrugged. 'Then I guess we just have to bide our time –' he couldn't resist a final dig, '– and hope that people don't forget you. Hollywood has a short memory.'

'They won't forget,' she replied, 'as you'll see at our party at the end of the month. Anyone who's anyone will be there.'

'A party, is it?' Fabio rubbed his hands together. 'If there's one thing nobody could forget it's the sort of shindig you guys used to throw.' He looked at Nayland. 'Why didn't you tell me?'

'I didn't know.'

'Did I forget to mention it?' Elizabeth smiled and offered her best attempt at 'coy'. It made Nayland think of a panther eyeing up the grisly remains of a gazelle. 'I'm such a scatterbrain.'

In fact, she had only just decided on the idea. As

Fabio had rightly pointed out, their parties had been legendary in the business and if there was a better way of making herself feel important again she didn't know of it.

'Well, you know I like a good party,' said Fabio, 'so at least one important mover and shaker will be there!' Neither Elizabeth or Nayland deemed that worth a reply. 'I might bring a new client of mine. Lovely boy.' He glanced at Elizabeth. 'You'd like him, I'm sure. He's going to be huge . . .'

'I hate him already,' Nayland replied, not altogether joking.

'The world will always be full of bright young things,' Fabio said. 'You can't put your foot down on Wilshire Boulevard without stepping on a beautiful face.'

'All the more reason to wear heels.' Elizabeth smiled around the filter of a cigarette and both men wondered whether she meant to eat it or smoke it.

'Those things will kill you, so I hear,' said Fabio, who smoked like a chimney himself.

'Darling,' Elizabeth said, smiling, '*nothing* could kill me.'

Fabio left finally, after he'd persuaded Patience to provide them with a couple of jugs of fruit punch and bored both Nayland and Elizabeth to distrac - tion with his pompous tales of life at the cutting edge of Hollywood business. Most of his stories were bullshit – actors knew that easily enough when they heard it (after all, they produced enough of it themselves) – but they let him talk. For all Elizabeth and Nayland's apparent indifference, the idea that the agent or manager was king was something still bred into them. You got nowhere in this business if the suits took a dislike to you. Hollywood was a puppet show, with people like Fabio holding the strings.

'I'll see you at the party,' he called, marching back through the house and towards the front door, a strutting walk that indicated he had things to do, business deals to strike. 'Let me know the date and time and I'll help spread the word.'

His driver, a long-suffering Pole called Teodor, snapped to attention when he saw his boss appear. He dashed around to open the passenger door, managing just in time as Fabio's pace didn't slow from doorway to steps to the inside of the big black Daimler: it was all the same world to him.

He gave one last wave before telling Teodor to take him back into town.

'Look at them,' he said to himself, watching Elizabeth and Nayland step back inside their house, 'wanting the whole world on a plate but never willing to put themselves out.' This wasn't altogether charitable, of course, especially since they had played host to him for the last hour or so, but if there was one thing managers hated it was their clients: life would go so much easier without them. 'Fucking vampires,' he muttered and turned back to watch the road ahead.

With the enforced conviviality gone from the house, Elizabeth and Nayland were left in the cold silence of the hall. Nayland tried to think of something to say that didn't have a barb in it but the words wouldn't come. Eventually Elizabeth just walked back out to the patio and he followed, cursing himself for falling into the role of the faithful hound, trotting along behind her.

'A party, then?' he asked, phrasing the words as non-judgementally as he could.

'A party,' she agreed, pouring the last of the fruit punch into her glass. 'You don't mind?'

Nayland shrugged. He *did* mind: he knew what happened at her parties and he had long ago tired of them.

'Oh, don't be such an old prude,' Elizabeth sighed, knowing full well – indeed, relishing – the fact that he disapproved. She fixed a venomous smile on her face, having decided that it might amuse her to goad him a little. 'Why do you always try and get in the way of me enjoying myself?'

'I hardly do that,' he replied, 'as you proved earlier.'

She feigned confusion for a moment. 'You mean the boys? We were just having a little fun.'

'Is that what you call it?'

'Yes, that *is* what I call it. So would you if you learned to unwind a little rather than walk around with that stiff British stick up your ass.' She paused. 'There was a time when you used to enjoy it yourself. Not with me, obviously, but you had friends of your own.'

'I just wish you could be a little more . . .' The words failed him.

'A little more what? Discreet? Or virginal? I'll never be either.'

'That much is clear.'

'Perhaps you would like it if we shared my little adventures.' Elizabeth leaned back, parting her legs a little, trying intentionally to anger him. 'Would that make it easier for you to stomach? I don't mind sharing, you know. I might even let you have a taste of what it is that you're so hungry for.'

Nayland's mouth curled into a scowl and she laughed.

'Perhaps not, then. I don't think I could sleep with someone who was disgusted with me.'

He clenched his fists, tired of being toyed with. 'If that were true, darling,' he said, getting to his feet, 'I doubt you'd ever find anyone to share your bed.'

He walked away from the table, reassuring himself that, whatever backbone he might have lacked, he still knew how to make a strong exit.

'You little shit!' Elizabeth roared, not even for

one moment willing to let him have the last word. 'Not everyone looks at me like you do! They adore me, you stuck-up little fool! They're lucky to be able to touch me!'

'Then why do you need to pay them?' Nayland asked, stepping back inside the house just as she threw her glass at him. A shower of glass fragments ricocheted off the door frame and the punch splashed against the panes of the French windows, exploding out into a Modernist painting done in blood-red.

'Bastard!' she screamed after him. But he kept walking.

Patience heard the sound of breaking glass and resigned herself to 'another one of those days'. Working for Elizabeth and Nayland was like being a governess for a pair of unruly children, trying to deal with the mood swings of one and the constant sulking of the other.

She beckoned over one of the maids, taking her away from where she was vacantly sweeping around the corners of the dining room. 'Outside, dear,' she said. 'Dustpan and brush. Get in and out as quickly as you can and do try to avoid getting under the mistress's feet. When she's in one of her tempers she's likely to tread on you.'

'Yes, ma'am,' the maid replied, making no further comment nor even expressing any sign of an opinion. This was good in Patience's book: as far as she was concerned, maids should be nothing more than ambulatory brooms, tools deployed silently and practically to perform a task. Still, this girl was more mindless than most. Patience tried to remember where she had come from. Not in the least bit interested in the lives of her staff outside their duties, the information was slow to surface. She had a vague memory of a poor family, a Catholic father who didn't altogether approve of his daughter working in such surroundings. Patience could understand that: Hollywood was peopled entirely with egos and sinners, which was what made it such a fertile feeding ground for the dreams of those who made their business there. If she had a daughter – which she didn't and never would have – then she was by no means sure she would allow her to be in service in such a home.

Elizabeth raged hard. She was a woman of excessive emotions, all of them stored right on the surface. No doubt that was what had made her such a successful silent-screen actress: her ability to show exactly what she was feeling in every glance or movement.

Sometimes, in rare and sometimes drunken moments of sincerity, she admitted that her temper was a failing. It burned too hot and consumed every bit of her. She claimed that it was the product of a hard childhood in Hungary, a life of abuse and penury. A childhood lived in fear of the whims and violence of a father whose name she never gave. In truth this was as false a legend as the one Fabio had woven around her when she first started working in the industry. It was an excuse. A cover story. Elizabeth had always been angry, her long-suffering mother would have said, wanting to roar at the world from her very first breath.

The anger gripped her painfully tight, suffocated her, constricted her. It made her feel as though lashing out was the only way to draw a breath. As she threw her glass at Nayland it offered the tiniest mouthful of cool air to a drowning woman. It wasn't enough. She threw his glass next, loving the way it exploded against the brick above the doors. Then she reached for a heavy fruit-punch jug, a weighty and satisfying weapon to throw at the world.

She hurled it as hard as she could, aiming for the glass of the French windows, wanting to fill the air with noise and destruction. Wanting to punch the whole damn world in its stupid, stupid mouth.

She had no idea that the maid would appear in the doorway the minute the jug left her grip, though even if she had known there was no guarantee she would have stayed her hand.

The jug hit the window and once more the air filled with broken glass. The maid screamed. Patience would have been relieved to see such a sudden sign of life on the witless girl's face. She dropped her broom and dustpan and they clattered to the floor as she raised her hands to her face in an attempt to protect herself from the sharp fragments. She was too slow – the first wave of glass flew at her face and wide-open mouth, cutting off her scream.

'Stupid girl!' Elizabeth shouted, not so much concerned with the maid's safety as with the potential consequences for the household of her being seriously hurt.

She ran to the window as the maid fell to the ground. Fruit splattered around her – orange slices, apple quarters, juicy strawberries exploding against the wall like the after-effect of gunfire.

Elizabeth grabbed at the girl, rolling her onto her back and then crying out herself as a gush of blood hit her in the eye. This sudden attack on her person was almost enough to force the rage further and she was a moment away from punching the girl when Patience arrived, fast but calm, bringing to the situation an authority that Elizabeth resented.

'Leave it to me, madam,' said Patience, pressing her hand to the maid's throat where a small shard had nicked the vein enough to cause the spray of blood that had hit Elizabeth.

Patience wasn't medically trained but she'd seen enough in her years of service to know a vein from an artery, a mess from a fatality. The maid, perhaps thankfully, had all but fainted, giving only a low groan as Patience brushed the glass from her face, neck and chest. One deep cut to the cheek, she noted, and one to the neck. It was the neck wound that could have turned the day into a disaster but it was bleeding gently and steadily, not pumping rhythmically like a severed artery. The wounded cheek would probably leave her with a scar – what might her father think of that?

Patience looked at her mistress, standing silent and spent behind her, half her face stained with the maid's blood. 'I can manage this, madam,' she insisted. 'If you would be good enough to send one of the other maids out I'll call the doctor and have her seen to.'

'She shouldn't have just stepped out,' said Elizabeth, still determined to make this anyone else's fault but her own. 'How could I have known it would hit her?'

Patience might have pointed out that if her mistress had refrained from hurling glassware around the place she would scarcely have had to concern herself about collateral damage. But comments like that are not the sort of thing that keep a woman in employment.

'It's all right, madam,' she replied. 'Everything will be fine. I will have the doctor take care of her. Just an accident.'

'Stupid girl,' Elizabeth muttered and, in a slight daze, she wandered back inside the house.

Patience bit her lower lip. There were times when she positively hated that woman.

Nayland heard the sound of breaking glass as he ran downstairs but he didn't let it trouble him. Let the woman shout and scream, let her tear the whole house down if she wanted to, he would neither stop her nor care. She was poison. An infection in his system that was eroding his insides as surely as the most debilitating disease. He might not be able to cure himself of it but he would, for now, remove himself from its direct influence.

At the bottom of the stairway he made his way along the short white corridor to the double doors of their projection room. When they had bought the place this had been his one and only stipulation. A private little theatre where he could screen movies, not just his own – while many actors, Elizabeth included, might be so egocentric as to do this his love was for the medium as a whole rather than his own magnified face – but anything that took his fancy. He researched his roles here, kept up with the latest hits and also revisited favourites from a private collection that rivalled any other.

Some people worked in this industry because they loved themselves, some because they loved money. For Nayland there was also a deep abiding love of the medium itself.

He had seen his first moving picture in 1914.

Hiding in America, desperate to distance himself from the horrors of the burgeoning war in Europe, a war that his younger brothers had gone off to fight, he had been struggling to make a career on the American stage. He had inflated his account of his successes in Britain, relying on the fact that the producers on Broadway wouldn't know a lie from the truth. The challenge was simple: if he wasn't a good enough actor to convince them of his bona fides then he didn't deserve the success. Armed with a collection of press clippings and a couple of letters of introduction (one forged) he had tried to force his way into any meeting he could. Hoping that his accent, his confidence and his looks would buy him the career he wanted.

So far it had singularly failed to do so.

One wet afternoon, seeking to hide from the rain, he had bought a ticket from the miserable manager sitting in the booth of the Roxy and had made his way into the dark auditorium, hoping for some -thing to take his mind off things.

The movie had been Griffith's *The Avenging Conscience*, overwrought, overlong and hampered by a fatal loss of faith in the final reel. In that, it might fairly have been said to accurately reflect life. Nayland cared not one jot about its shortcomings: he was utterly transfixed by it. This was a new world, a new grammar, a new way of telling stories. He loved cinema's tricks: the split screen, the dream sequence and, most particularly, the way it forced the audience's attention in a specific direction. On stage you built images, offered tableaux and set effects but you were always hampered by the fact that you were being viewed from all angles, maybe not even viewed at all if an audience member took that opportunity to be distracted by some other piece of movement. You couldn't take them and shove their faces in the essence of it. That was the major strength of cinema, he believed. The actor wants you to see his response to the venomous proclamations of his uncle? Well then, here it is, filling the whole screen, every detail, every ounce of hatred and recrimination. It was a revelation for Nayland and his love of live theatre vanished that very afternoon, trodden underfoot among the discarded takeout containers and cigarette ends.

He had made his slow way towards Los Angeles, paying his way en route with whatever disposable labour he could offer. Once on the West Coast his fortunes were quick to change: he had the face and charm for the movie industry and, most impor-tantly, the camera loved him. An actor who had been overshadowed on the stage, lost in the shadow of bigger, more assured performances, had found his natural home. Rendered large on the screen he had what could never be faked: a beauty and magnetism that made audiences love him.

Women wanted him, men wanted to be him. Within twelve months he had gone from a washed-up stage actor to a screen icon. Through it all he never lost his love for cinema. If anything, knowing the off-screen tricks – the camera techniques, the lighting methods – thrilled him even more. Cinema wasn't a miracle, it was magic that anyone could learn and duplicate. Nayland had found his perfect home. Just look where it had got him.

The little projection room had seats for thirty, with the projector booth a small raised room reached by a spiral staircase at the back. He climbed up to it, and worked his way through the large storage cupboard that held his collection. He already knew what he wanted to see, though he half hoped that his gaze would fall on something else, something more escapist, as he ran his fingers along the edge of the film canisters. But it didn't. Here was *The Golden Cockerel*, a melodrama set in the Deep South, telling the tale of two families at war. *Romeo and Juliet* reworked for a cast of honest toilers in dungarees and straw hats. It had been the first film in which he had appeared with Elizabeth. He had played Jed, the eldest son of the Capstan clan, she Viola, the rose in the flower bed of the Jackson family tree.

Nayland skipped the first couple of reels, want - ing to cut to the chase. Loading up the projector he set it to run and climbed back down to the auditorium, taking a seat in the front row where the screen loomed so large that it blanked out everything else.

There she was, dressed down in homespun gingham, her hair pulled into twin plaits. Her face was so beautiful, the lines of excess and abuse as yet unformed. When she smiled her lips stretched several feet to either side and he wanted nothing more than to strip off and climb inside that mouth, to lie back on her soft tongue and feel her hot breath wash over him.

Here was the perfection that he could never find in the real world. Here was the Elizabeth Sasdy that could only be known on film. She never spoke, communicating through intertitles that offered none of the harsh edge her voice had in real life. 'Oh Jed,' the screen translated, 'how I wish you'd just hold me!' and he had and would still if only this perfect vision walked the Earth.

Nayland watched his screen self kiss that simple, beautiful hybrid of Viola and Elizabeth and tried to recall how those lips had felt. He hadn't known what crimes they were capable of back then: they had simply enchanted him, excited him, made him determined to have her.

The memory of her brought him to life in his seat and he leaned back and unbuckled his trousers. There was a moment of shame, then Elizabeth looked directly at the camera, offering that brooding, sultry look that had stiffened half the audiences back in the late 1920s and made her a bankable legend. He was as vulnerable now as he had been then – as *everyone* had been then. He filled his palm and, eyes fixed on the only true love of his life, imagined being able to enter this most perfect vision of her. A shining monochrome lover, moving jerkily astride him as the film was hand-cranked through the camera. Would she carry the scent of the film if he pressed his face into her neck? Would her skin have its smooth, cool touch? As he pushed himself into her he imagined the heat from between their legs exposing the image, a snapshot of where their bodies met, coming into perfect focus before the heat burned the film as white as the sun.

'I love you, Jed.' Her words appeared on the screen as he came. 'And I always will.'

Suddenly exposed, his passion reduced to a cooling groin and spilled seed he had no idea what to do with, he found himself more depressed than ever. Above him Elizabeth Sasdy looked down and give a sparkling, coquettish laugh.

The real Elizabeth was not smiling. She was sitting in her room, staring at herself in the mirror. She had been doing so for some time, trapped in her own head, unable to break the seemingly unshakeable connection between her eyes and those of her reflection. The room was quiet but inside her head it was all about the sound of breaking glass. At that moment, it seemed to her, with blood on her face, that she looked more beautiful than she had for years. Was *this* the real Elizabeth? A dangerous and violent creature, a woman who wore the blood of others like face paint? Yes, she thought, it just might be.

But she could hardly stay that way for ever. She went to the bathroom and slowly and methodically bathed the blood away. It had begun to dry and, with the dab of a wet flannel, it became liquid once more, trickling down her cheek towards her chin. A thin rivulet caught on her lower lip and she decided to embrace her new animal state by licking at it, tasting the violence. It was surprisingly innocuous – perhaps she needed more of it to truly appreciate the flavour.

Eventually her face was clean and she stared at it for some time, trying to decide whether her eyes were deceiving her. Was this momentary madness colouring her vision or had the blood wrought an impossible effect on her skin? She had been looking at this face only hours ago, though in truth she needn't have refreshed the memory so recently because she knew every line and crease, knew the way her cheeks had sunk just as the rest of her had swelled. She had been following the slow descent from perfection, like an endless horror novel she couldn't stop herself from reading with the turn of each new page. This was not her face. No . . . that was not true, it was her face, but her face as it *had* been, not as it now was. She only had to compare it with the area around it, the parts of her visage that had not been touched by the maid's blood. Where the blood had been the lines were gone, the skin was tighter, fresher, *younger*. An impossibility. She might have been a poor girl from Hungary but that didn't make her a fool, something of which she often felt the need to remind people. This could not have happened. And yet denying it was the greatest foolishness of all. It was right there in front of her: one side of her face was markedly younger than the other, the face of a woman twenty years her junior. The face that she had originally brought to this godless city, the face it had fallen in love with like so many before it. But how?

She thought of the tales she had heard when young. Stories told by her mother to fill out the dark hours between food and sleep. She remembered in particular the countess who had shared her first name, Elizabeth Báthory, the woman who had thrilled and terrified people for generations after her with the hundreds of deaths attributed to her. She had supposedly bathed in the blood of virgins to retain her youth, a female counterpart to Vlad the Impaler. A beast, a fiend, a human vampire.

But surely there could be no truth in it? Oh, certainly the woman had ordered the deaths of hundreds of young girls, and maybe she had even allowed herself the luxury of bathing in their still-warm blood. But there could be no real effect, could there?

Then how do you explain what you can see with your own eyes? said a voice inside her head. *Are you so changed by this new America, this land of reason and science, that you deny the truth of what you can see before you?*

Elizabeth rubbed at the renewed cheek, firm and sculpted. It could lie to her fingers no more than it could to her eyes: it was the cheek of a much younger woman.

Her heart pounding, her hands automatically reached for one of her tranquillisers. She stopped herself. When had she become so afraid of strong emotion that she felt the need to medicate against it? Let her heart pound. Let her breathing quicken. She was looking at a miracle and what other response could there be to such a thing?

Then came the thought that triggered everything that came after, the thought that sealed not only her fate but also those of the innocents that would follow. A simple thought. A logical thought. A terrible, terrible thought.

But what about the rest of me?

Patience lived up to her name. She had cleaned the maid's wounds and the doctor had visited, dismissing the matter as of no great concern (as much because of the social status of the patient as the relative mildness of her wounds). He had put a few stitches in her cheek but was confident that it would heal cleanly.

'It's hardly the end of the world,' he had said, taking his leave. 'She should just get back to work.'

A sentiment with which Patience wholly sympathised. If only to shut the stupid girl up.

'I've never seen anyone so angry,' the girl said, still sitting in the dining room as if waiting for further attention. 'I thought she was going to kill me. The look in her eyes . . .'

'She and the master had been fighting,' Patience explained for the umpteenth time. 'You know how couples get when they don't see eye to eye.'

'Well,' the girl replied, 'I suppose, not that I've got a husband . . .'

Patience was not in the least surprised.

'Daddy says there's time enough for all of that later,' the maid continued, 'when I'm older and want to settle down.' She looked up at her nurse. 'Not that I'm exactly unsettled now, I'm always at this house or at home. You know what it's like.'

Patience lived in so could only envy the girl her occasional escape. Nonetheless she nodded.

'Of course, if I had money . . .' And with that the girl's face changed and Patience's heart sank. It was to be like this, was it? The maid's getting caught in the crossfire between her employers was not a misfortune, it was an opportunity. All these kids were the same, always looking for a short cut.

'Patience?'

The woman looked up to see her employer in the doorway. Elizabeth still looked dishevelled: her hair, normally worn up, had been allowed to hang down, unbrushed, over half of her face. She looks like a demon, Patience thought, in uncharacteristically dramatic terms.

'Yes, ma'am?'

'How is the girl?' Elizabeth entered and, on seeing the maid sitting in one of her dining chairs, her face lit up with what Patience would have called concern had she seen the expression on the face of any person other than her mistress. 'There you are!'

The maid shrank back, unable to stop herself cowering slightly.

'I'm so sorry,' Elizabeth continued, 'I have been beside myself with worry. To think how close I came to . . . It doesn't bear thinking about.'

'No, ma'am,' the maid said, glad they had at least one thing they could agree on.

'You must think terribly of me,' Elizabeth continued. Patience tensed at that, knowing full well that if there was one sure-fire way to ignite the anger of her employer it would be agreement.

'Of course not, ma'am,' the maid replied. 'You were just angry. I know that. You didn't mean to hurt me.'

'Indeed not – in fact, we must make sure we take good care of you.' Elizabeth bent down and stroked the girl's face, running the pad of her thumb just below the cut on her cheek. The girl winced slightly but it wasn't enough to take her mind off the promise of what her employer had said.

'I'm sure you will,' she said. Patience was dismayed at the bare greed she saw on the girl's face. She wasn't even bothering to hide it. 'I know you and the master are fine Christian folk.'

Elizabeth laughed at that – how could she not? 'I don't know about that,' she said, 'but we will certainly make sure you don't feel badly treated. Have you plans for the evening?'

This question wrong-footed the girl, so unexpected was it. 'No,' she admitted. 'In fact, I was just saying to Miss Patience that I never really do much outside work.'

'Well, tonight you shall,' said Elizabeth. 'You will be my guest here and we will see if we can't give you a night to remember.'

The maid was actually concerned by the idea of that. 'Oh, I couldn't impose!'

'Nonsense! And it's no imposition. You will stay the night with us and we will see what we can do to entertain you. Besides, we need to talk about what manner of compensation we need to give you.'

And again, greed obscured any more rational thought. 'I don't know what to say . . .'

If I were you, Patience suddenly thought, *I would say no*.

But the maid was not her. 'I can't believe it!' Embarrassment got in the way again. 'But I haven't got anything to wear . . . Oh Lord . . . it wouldn't be right. I'm only staff . . . I shouldn't be . . .'

Elizabeth took both the girl's hands. 'Nonsense. What's the difference, really? Why, only a few years ago I was no more important than you.'

Patience had her job cut out not to let her expression respond to that somewhat backhanded compliment. Graciousness had never come easily to the mistress, nor humility. Patience was quite sure that Elizabeth Sasdy had never considered herself unimportant.

'Why don't you come with me and we'll see what we can find for you?'

Elizabeth lifted the maid to her feet and, starry-eyed, the girl looked back at Patience as if she was seeking permission. What right had she to offer an opinion either way? Patience had no doubt that nothing good could come from the mistress's mood but she could hardly say so.

She just nodded and watched the girl being led away.

*

'We could go out,' Elizabeth was saying, though Georgina, the maid, barely heard her. She simply couldn't believe what was happening to her and everything had taken on the distant, dislocated feeling of a dream.

'Have drinks somewhere, then back here for dinner, something special . . . something fabulous!'

'There's really no need,' Georgina insisted, utterly overwhelmed.

'Oh, bless you.' Elizabeth pulled her close and kissed her on her unwounded cheek. 'There's every need. I've treated you terribly and I simply couldn't live with myself unless I made it up to you.'

She led the girl into her dressing room, a place bigger even than her bedroom, a mirror-lined chamber of concealed wardrobes. The outfits con - tained therein formed a museum of her public appearances: gowns and frocks, skirts and blouses, many of them worn only once and then filed away as a memento.

'You're a little more petite than me,' Elizabeth noted, 'but I'm sure we can find something that will work.'

Georgina could barely hold still in the room, shifting awkwardly from one foot to another as she turned around and around, being chased by her ever-present reflection. She was an animal utterly removed from her environment and with no idea how to adapt. 'I'm sure nothing here would be right. I wouldn't know how to wear it.'

'Oh darling, any woman can wear anything. Now, get rid of that uniform and let's see what we can find.'

'Get rid . . .?'

'Don't be shy – you can hardly wear a frock over the top of it, can you? We're all girls together.'

'I suppose so.' Reluctantly, Georgina reached behind her and began to untie her pinny.

'Besides,' continued Elizabeth, 'today that is no longer who you are: no more service, no more uniform, just the beauty beneath it.'

'Beauty?' Georgina looked at her reflection and scowled at what she saw. 'I'm no beauty.'

Elizabeth had to agree as the girl unzipped her black dress to expose a pale, thin body underneath. *Just look at this creature*, she thought, *with her hairy arms and legs, her jutting knees and flat chest, her mismatched underwear and her skin like curdled milk. What loss was such a thing? What a small price to pay in a world where beauty was everything.*

Out loud Elizabeth was the consummate actress: 'Nonsense! The waif look is the next thing. I'm so jealous! Look at my pudgy body compared to yours, so lean and toned.'

'Toned?'

'Fit, supple.'

'Oh, that'll be the sweeping, I suppose. It really takes it out of you, especially on the hot days.'

'I just bet it does.'

Elizabeth pulled out a red satin dress. She had worn it for the premiere of *Starlings*, a Southern Gothic where she had played an abandoned orphan looking after younger children in the cruel home where they had been abandoned. She had lost weight for the role: the director had been deter-mined to capture the look of a young woman who had survived off little but oats and raw potatoes for most of her life. She had hated the movie but the critics hadn't and that had been the important thing. What she saw as unnecessary torture had been lauded as 'dazzling commitment to the role'. Fabio had been quick to release to the papers how she had been eager to experience the discomfort of the many real-life unfortunates who grew up in a state of abuse and fear, and hinted that a portion of her fee was going to a local orphanage. It hadn't, naturally – Elizabeth would never have stood for such waste. But the press had done her no end of favours, even when she had been photographed gorging herself at the premiere party, finally able to stuff herself with platters of cold meats and creamed potatoes.

'Try this,' she suggested, holding the frock out to Georgina.

'Oh that's just . . .' The words wouldn't come easily to the girl. 'I mean . . . it's *wonderful*.'

'I think you'll look fabulous in it,' Elizabeth assured her. 'If only your boyfriend could see you in it, eh?'

'I haven't got a boyfriend,' Georgina admitted. She looked uncomfortable at the admission though not so much that she wasn't willing to go further. 'There was one boy, I thought he loved me . . . he wanted . . . well, you know what boys always want. But then I never saw him for dust.'

'Oh, men are such pigs,' said Elizabeth, 'though there's nothing wrong with a bit of pleasure from time to time! God wouldn't have given us our bodies unless he wanted us to use them, now would he?'

'I suppose not. I never really thought about it like that.' The girl looked at Elizabeth, clearly weighing up whether to say any more. 'I gave him what he wanted,' she eventually confessed, 'and it was nice, I suppose, though he obviously didn't think so as he never hung around for more.'

Interesting, thought Elizabeth. *Not a virgin, then. Thank God for that. I mean, where the hell do you get virgins in this town?*

Georgina struggled into the dress with Elizabeth's help, lost in the soft fabric and the awkwardly placed buttons.

'I never . . .' The girl looked at herself in the mirror and actually started to cry. 'I've never worn such a thing, never looked so . . .'

She looks like a child playing at dress-up, thought Elizabeth, *utterly at odds with the clothes, like a head being cut from one photo and stuck on another*.

'Now we need to do your hair and make-up,' she told the girl, 'to make you perfect.'

'Perfect,' Georgina repeated. 'I never thought I could be perfect.'

Neither did I, Elizabeth agreed. *Not again . . . but with your help . . .*

Nayland spent a little while in the screening room, calming himself down with some Mack Sennett shorts. If he could have stayed down there for ever he would certainly have done so. Let them all go about their stupid games without him. Here he had the best of them all, the perfect versions, the ones who would never let you down as long as the film still rolled and the light still burned.

But rise up he must, and if he did so then let him absorb as much good humour from the foolish antics of Billy Bevan, Ben Turpin and the lovely Alice Day as he could.

The house was quiet when he ascended into the entrance hall, with nothing but a slightly perturbed look on Patience's face to alert him that all might not be well.

'Something wrong?' he asked.

'Nothing, I'm sure, sir,' she replied. 'There was a slight accident with one of the maids. The mistress was –' Nayland saw her struggle for the least emotive words she could find, '– agitated, and she threw some glassware.'

'Indeed she did, at me.'

'It hit a maid and I'm afraid she was hurt.'

'Badly?'

'The doctor says not.' There was a discernible and weighted pause. 'Though the mistress seems determined to make it up to the girl. I believe she said something about taking her out dancing.'

And now Nayland could see why Patience was concerned. Elizabeth was not a gracious woman.

'Dancing?'

'Yes, sir.'

'Then everything sounds fine, doesn't it?' He made it clear that there was only one correct answer.

'Absolutely, sir. I shall go about my duties.'

'Indeed.'

Nayland went upstairs, dreading what he might find.

'Let's make ourselves beautiful!' said Elizabeth.

'What do you mean?' asked Georgina, as if the concept was still beyond her grasp.

'I mean we need to bathe, do our hair and make-up and douse ourselves in scent that the men will find irresistible!'

'Oh.' Georgina looked down at her dress. 'So I have to take this off again?'

'Only for now, darling, only for now.'

Elizabeth's main bathroom lay directly off the dressing room. If there was one thing she didn't believe in it was skimping on the space available for pampering. She slid back a large mirrored panel to reveal a spacious tub and shower.

'My word!' said Georgina. 'It's lovely, and so big.'

'Indeed it is,' Elizabeth agreed. She had tested its capacity with visiting guests on many occasions – in fact, she couldn't remember the last time she had bathed in it alone. Nor would she tonight.

'Never cut back on the important things in life,' she said with a smile, heading over to the tub and putting the plug in place. Her hand automatically reached for the tap but she stopped herself. She didn't want to run the water, not yet.

Georgina was clearly feeling uncomfortable, standing in the bathroom in nothing but her cheap underwear. 'I think I'd lose myself in it,' she said.

Maybe you will, Elizabeth thought.

For a moment she thought about what she was planning. Was she really intending to go through with this? Her concerns were not about morality, a diluted concept after years of living her lifestyle. It was a word to be found in dictionaries, something that existed elsewhere, like the poverty and hunger that she had risen above.

The only question in her mind was: *Can I get away with this? Can I get what I want and then walk away scot-free?* It said more about her arrogance than her planning skills that she decided the answer was yes. She could do what she wanted: she was Elizabeth Sasdy, Queen of Hollywood.

She stepped behind Georgina so that she was between the girl and the door. 'No need to be shy,' she said. 'I'll leave you to it once I've shown you where everything is.'

Pleased to see that this made the girl relax a little, Elizabeth moved over to the bathroom cabinets. She opened the heavy pearlescent doors to reveal stacks of white towels. Then the next cabinet was opened to show an array of soaps, powders and shampoos. Elizabeth reached in and pulled out a selection of bottles, throwing them one at a time to Georgina.

'This is wonderful – California citrus, smells like you're bathing in a lemon tree. This one is supposed to be good for your skin. This is for your hair. This is a scented conditioner.'

Georgina, struggling to hold all the bottles, terri - fied of dropping one, looked at the object that Elizabeth still had in her hand. 'And what's that for?'

'This, dear?' asked Elizabeth, opening the cut-throat razor. 'This is for making me look young again.'

She moved behind the girl, slapping a hand firmly across her mouth to stop the inevitable scream.

Georgina kept hold of the bottles even as she realised what was about to happen, her instinct not to damage things that weren't hers bred into her so deeply that it helped cost her her life. Not that she would have had time to do much, anyway – Elizabeth was quick, drawing the blade across her throat as her father had done with the pigs back in Hungary: one sure cut. Then she pushed the girl forward so that she fell into the bath, the bottles clattering around her feet.

Georgina hit the enamelled surface with a dull thud, her hands slapping at the bath as she tried to push herself up. Her palms splayed in the blood that was gushing from her. However hard she fought for a breath so that she could scream, the wound in her throat wouldn't let her.

Elizabeth closed and locked the bathroom door only moments before Nayland appeared on its other side.

'Elizabeth?' he shouted. 'Are you all right? It sounded like something fell over.'

Georgina was still now, the only sound that of the pumping spray of blood against the inside of the bath. A repetitive soft slap against the enamel.

'I'm fine,' Elizabeth said. 'Like you care.'

She undid her dressing gown, not wanting to get blood on it, then stepped forward, straddling Georgina so she could lift her up and squeeze more blood from the gash in her throat.

'About earlier,' said Nayland, 'what I said . . . I'm sorry, I just get . . .'

'I know what you get,' she replied. Christ, did he have to try and have a heart-to-heart now? This was hardly a convenient time. 'Look.' She set Georgina back down as the flow of blood slowed to a trickle. 'We'll talk later, all right?'

A pause. 'OK.' A longer pause. 'Is the maid with you?'

Patience had been talking, Elizabeth realised. 'Of course she isn't – I'm taking a bath. I gave her fifty dollars and told her to take the night off.'

'Patience seemed to think you were going to take her out . . . dancing.'

Elizabeth laughed. 'Does that sound like me?'

'No,' Nayland had to admit. 'I was surprised.'

'I told you, I gave her some money and packed her off. Now go away – we'll talk later.'

'Fine.' There was a shuffling on the other side of the door while Nayland decided if there was any - thing else he could say. He realised there wasn't and she listened to him walk away slowly, closing the dressing-room door behind him. Finally, peace.

She went back to Georgina and lifted her up by the ankles. Elizabeth was a strong woman and certainly not averse to flexing her muscles. Still, she was glad the girl had been so slight. She squeezed the maid's body, trying to work as much of the blood as possible out of it. There was always going to be wastage, she decided, maybe a couple of pints retained by the body despite her best efforts.

Looking down into the bath she decided there was more than enough. If one small splash had had such a pronounced effect how could all this not revitalise her completely?

But what if its potency faded after death?

Elizabeth grabbed a large sponge, climbed into the tub, squatted down and got to work.

The blood was cooling quickly. She dragged the loaded sponge up her legs, the skin glowing with warmth to begin with before quickly chilling off. Then she rubbed it across her shoulders and chest, letting the liquid run down. She dropped back so that she was sitting in the thick puddle, working fast to paint every inch of herself, forcing the sponge into every hated fold and crease. The blood thickened on her as it began to clot and dry, her limbs sticking to her torso as she tried to shift in the bath and become more comfortable.

She soaked up more on the sponge and squeezed it out over her head, massaging it into her hair and scalp and finally her face. She closed her eyes as lightly as she could and doused herself, letting the fluid run from her forehead in a dripping curtain. She used her fingers to rub the blood in, massaging her cheeks, pushing her fingers along the side of her nose, working the skin hard. She nearly choked as she accidentally snorted in a little, feeling it run down the back of her throat like salty syrup.

Her neck, too: no more sagging jowls or puckered throat. She rubbed and rubbed, dipping her hands into the blood beneath her and smear - ing herself all over, obsessively returning to every part of her that she had grown to hate, pinching and twisting the skin, letting her nails scrape at it, punishing it for being so weak, so pathetic and old.

Eventually, muscles aching and her whole body sticking to the bath beneath her, Elizabeth lay back and relaxed.

The smell was pungent but not unpleasant – she wanted to be reminded of the potency of what she was lying in, the animal richness of it.

How long did it take to work? Perhaps the longer she had it on her body the greater the effect? Though surely there was a limit? She could hardly shrink away back to childhood here in her slick second womb. Her skin tingled, though whether that was from the rough attention she'd paid it or whether it was proof that the blood was taking effect she couldn't say.

She realised she'd been holding her breath and she let out a sigh that bubbled through wet lips.

She should be horrified. She should be disgusted. She didn't want to open her eyes – not because she was scared to look upon the literal bloodbath she had created but because she wanted her eyelids to receive the full benefit. She reached out a hand and rested it on the cool flank of the dead maid, the woman she had killed. She realised she felt nothing. No, not nothing, worse than that: she felt thrilled. She felt powerful. She felt back in a place of dominance, feeding off the little people, thriving off their devotion. She felt *herself*.

She waited for about twenty minutes, then decided that the blood must have done its work. She was too impatient to wait any longer.

Elizabeth sat up and reached out for the taps. In her head she briefly heard her father's voice. *'Cold water for blood,'* he said and she could picture him hurling bucket after bucket of icy water on the bloodstained floor of the barn after he had slaughtered one of the pigs. *'It chills it off the stones.'*

She had no idea whether there was any truth to that but decided there was little point in arguing.

She turned on the cold-water tap and let the liquid rush out. She gave an involuntary shriek as it splashed on her, cupping it with both hands nonetheless and pouring it over her head, letting it rush over her shoulders. A cloud of pink blos - somed around her as the blood began to be washed off. She removed the plug and swirled the blood residue away, forcing it down the outlet.

Leaning over the side of the bath she nudged Georgina's legs aside so that she could reach for one of the bottles she had handed her, the shampoo. Elizabeth poured a good handful into her hair and massaged it, constantly cupping more cold water and dousing herself with it.

It took a long time but eventually she was clean.

She stood up and, on impulse, turned her gaze away from the bathroom mirror. She didn't want this piecemeal, she wanted to appreciate the full effect.

She stepped out into her dressing room and stared at herself in the mirrors that surrounded her.

She was beautiful. Perfect. A woman who had lost twenty years . . . more, even. She couldn't take her stare off herself. Her hands constantly stroked her body, feeling every inch of its rejuvenation.

A miracle. And one that was certainly worth the life of a stupid maid, a girl whom nobody in their right mind would miss.

Which was when she noticed the girl's uniform, still discarded on the floor. Had Nayland seen it? No matter if he had: he would keep her secret. She would make quite sure of that.

Nayland *had* noticed the uniform – had been staring at it, in fact, when he had asked Elizabeth about the girl's whereabouts.

'I gave her fifty dollars,' his wife had said, 'and told her to take the night off.'

A lie, surely. But hiding what truth?

He had retired to his own room. Once again lost

inside his own house, feeling out of control and powerless beneath a roof that increasingly felt like that of a prison rather than a home.

He poured himself a large Scotch and sat in the window, watching an unhealthy sun sink behind the mountains. Part of him wished it would have the decency to just stay there.

The maid. What had Elizabeth done to the maid?

And, more to the point, what was he going to do about it?

Nayland lost himself in the shadows, the faint light from a bedside lamp too thin to permeate further than the safety of his white-sheeted bed.

Elizabeth came to him a few hours later. A silhouette in his doorway, a ghost bathed in expensive scent.

'Look at you,' she said, 'sat staring out into the dark.'

'Story of my life.'

'It doesn't have to be.' She stepped inside the room and closed the door behind her. 'Turn off that light.'

He didn't question her – did he ever? – just got to his feet, walked over and let the darkness possess those last few steps.

'Take off your clothes.'

This did give him pause. Unsure for a moment whether it would be the prelude to humiliation. What the hell, it wasn't as if he had any pride left.

He dropped his garments to the floor, casting them into the darkness where they were lost.

He stood there in what little moonlight managed to filter in through the window, broken up and carved by the blades of the palm trees outside. He looked down at his body, a scratchy projection of his past self, a grainy monochrome print of a man.

'Close your eyes,' Elizabeth said.

'I can't see a thing anyway.'

'Close them.'

Nayland did so, forcing himself to relax, spreading out his hands and letting himself float in the darkness. Giving in to her as he always did. He heard her move closer, the soft breath of air as she came to him, the awareness of something else out there in this ocean of darkness, a big predator certainly, one that he had long ago accepted would one day eat him whole.

Elizabeth whispered in his ear. 'I'm going to do what I want.'

'When have you not?' he replied.

Her fingers brushed his chest, his cheeks, ran their nails down his arms, so lightly that it was like being touched by a spirit, something without flesh. The illusion would not be maintained for long. After a moment of absence, left to float once more, he felt her take hold of his penis, her thumbnail dragging its way along it, promising pain as well as pleasure.

'I've missed this,' Elizabeth told him. He didn't believe her, of course, but it was nice to hear. His body had no issue with her lies, and he stiffened between her fingers.

Nayland pictured her as he had seen her on the screen, imagined her hands reaching out from the projector's beam and pulling him in. She tugged him towards the bed, leading him like the obedient old hound that he was.

'Lie back,' she said, feet still planted on the floor, toes curling against the marble tiles.

The spirit of Elizabeth vanished to be replaced with the animal that lived at the heart of her. She climbed on top of Nayland, hands forcing him down against the sprung mattress as she rode him as though he was an inanimate object. As always, the goal was her pleasure but that didn't lessen his own. He gripped the sheets on either side of him and pressed his head back into the bed, stiffening at the scratching of her nails, the bite of her teeth, the hungry grind of her as she pounded against him. It was an act of vandalism and he loved her all the more for it.

Afterwards, she sat back among his pillows while he lay still, enjoying the feel of the cool air on his wet skin. He wanted to remember the sensation.

'Why?' Nayland asked, a question he hadn't wanted to raise earlier in case it had made her come to her senses.

'A celebration,' Elizabeth said. 'And a business proposition.'

'Where do I sign?'

'I think you just did.' She was silent for a moment. 'Do you have a cigarette?'

'Bedside table.' Nayland made to sit up, reaching for the light, but she pushed him back down with her foot.

'I can manage.' She scrabbled in the half-light, opening the cigarette case and helping herself. There was a flash of orange fire and then the air was filled with the scent of smoke, eradicating the afterglow aroma of their sex, fumigating them.

'I have not been happy,' she said after smoking in silence for a while. 'Not for a long time. Did you realise that?'

'Yes,' he admitted. 'But as you clearly didn't want me to do anything about it . . .'

'What could you have done?' It was not a question that Elizabeth expected him to answer. 'But if there had been a way, something that would have made me really happy, would you have done it?'

'You know I would. I'm an idiot, but I'm consistent.'

'You really love me, don't you?'

'Yes.' Nayland could see no point in lying – she knew it, anyway.

'Even though I treat you so terribly?'

'Yes.'

'Why?'

'I have no idea.'

'There is a way.'

'A way to what?'

'To make me happy. I found it tonight. But I need you to be a part of it.'

'The maid?'

'Yes, though probably not in the way you think.'

Nayland didn't want to hear more: this was the terror that waited on the next sunrise, the next step on the downward spiral. He knew she wouldn't spare him. 'What did you do?'

In answer Elizabeth reached across and turned on the bedside light. It took a moment for what he saw to sink in. He scooted across the bed to prop himself up against the footboard, staring at the woman facing him.

'What have you done?' he asked. 'What the hell have you done?'

'Something miraculous, and all it cost was the blood of someone unimportant.'

Someone unimportant. How mild those words were. How terrible.

'Tell me!'

'Darling, there's no need to shout. It was just an accident, a happy accident.'

'Not for her.'

'Oh, who cares about her? She was nothing, just a silly little girl. Since when have we had to worry about people like that? This is who we are, the gods of the screen, grown beautiful by feeding on them. All I did was take it a step further. Her blood made me beautiful. Am I not beautiful?'

Nayland couldn't deny that. She looked absolutely stunning, better even than she had in his screening room. She was the perfect dream of herself. The definitive Elizabeth.

'Of course you are.' He moved closer and she tilted her head, spreading her limbs out before him, soaking up all his attention.

'Did I ever look better?'

'No,' he admitted. 'But . . . the girl . . .'

'Is dead and there's nothing that can be done to bring her back. So why worry? We just need to get rid of the body.'

He sank back on the bed. 'We?'

'You wouldn't let me struggle on my own, would you? And you know I'd be grateful. I might even love you for it.'

'Don't promise what you can't deliver.'

'Who knows?'

Nayland knew only too well but he wasn't going to argue about it.

'Will you help?' Elizabeth rubbed her young toes on his old, grey chest. 'You wouldn't let me go to the chair over such a stupid little thing as this, would you?'

'I should.'

'But you won't.'

'No, God help me, I won't.'

'Good boy.'

They dressed, Nayland unable to stop staring at Elizabeth, she loving every moment of it.

'What are we going to say?' he asked.

'I told Patience that we were going to take her out. Who's to say what happened to her after we left her?'

'Not the maid. You. People won't believe it. You're so young . . .'

This had never occurred to Elizabeth, the idea that she had restored her beauty but wouldn't be able to show it. She looked at herself in the mirror. 'This is Hollywood – they'll believe anything we tell them. That's what they do. We're not human, we're not real . . . they expect miracles from us every day.'

'And Patience? Or Fabio?'

'Fabio will see dollar signs, Patience will just have to do as she's told. That's what she's for.' Elizabeth tore herself away from the mirror. 'We'll worry about that in the morning, one thing at a time.'

She led him into the bathroom. He saw the drained body of Georgina dumped in the tub.

'Oh God.' Nayland pressed his hand to his mouth, then said, 'Oh Elizabeth, what did you do?'

'What needed to be done.' She had brought in the red dress that she had promised Georgina she could wear. 'Help me get her into this.'

'Why, for God's sake?'

'Because it will look better. We dress her up and dump her. Stick to our story, that we took her out for dinner somewhere . . .'

'Where?'

'I don't know. Luciano's, Oceanic . . .'

'They'll check! The police will ask if we were there.' Nayland rubbed at his face, trying to force his brain into action. 'This needed planning, care . . . you just killed her and now . . .'

'I needed you,' Elizabeth purred. 'All right? I admit it. I should have asked you to help.'

'To help you kill.' He bent over, trying to get his breath. A world that had been loose enough already was falling apart around him.

'To help me get new life. Would you begrudge me that?'

Oh, but the cost . . . Nayland thought, looking at the dead eyes of their maid.

'It's done,' Elizabeth insisted. 'Now we need to fix it or I'll be joining her.' She fixed him with a stare so hard that he felt as if she had shoved him. 'And I will not accept that.'

He nodded. However much the act disgusted him she was right in that the girl's life was gone. Nothing he could do would change that. The choice had been made. Now he had to decide whether Elizabeth should pay for it or not. As always, he bowed to her.

'All right.' Nayland drew in a breath and forced himself to act. He grabbed the maid under her arms and lifted her from the tub. There was a loud belch and he dropped her again, with a cry of panic. 'She's not dead!'

'Of course she's dead. It's just gas. You remember that movie we did? *The Cedar Grove*? With Larry Michaels. He told me about the girl I was playing, the real one, how they had found her body in the pond and she had blown up like a Zeppelin. They'd never show that on-screen, of course, just me floating among the lilies. But real death is ugly.'

'It is indeed.' He picked Georgina up again. 'Pull the dress up her legs.'

Elizabeth did so, yanking the material over the girl's damp body. The girl seemed to fight back, Nayland straining to hold her still as her limbs flailed. It was like trying to dress a large marionette.

'Put her down,' said Elizabeth. 'I need to get her arms through.'

Nayland tried to rest the girl on the edge of the bath but she fell in, her head striking the enamel with a resounding bang.

'Careful!' said Elizabeth.

'What does it matter? She can't get any more dead – you've seen to that.'

'Just lift her back out.'

He did so, tugging her up by her arms, her head lolling on her thin neck.

Elizabeth stepped in between them, pulling the dress up and then taking hold of each arm to fold it through the straps. The left one seemed to fight back and the fabric ripped.

Elizabeth yelled a Hungarian curse, stepping back to take a swing at the dead girl. She slapped her across the face and Nayland had to yank hard to stop her from being torn from his grip.

'What are you doing?' he demanded. 'That's not helping.'

'Neither is she.'

'Just pull it around her, it'll be fine. Who cares if it's torn?'

Elizabeth did just that. 'She'll do. Now we need to get her out of the house.'

'I'll carry her to the garage, you walk ahead of me and make sure nobody sees us.' He hoisted her up onto his shoulder and a splatter of blood shot from her gashed throat and ran down the back of his jacket.

'Shit!' He turned around, trying to see how bad it was in the mirror.

'The material's dark enough,' Elizabeth insisted. 'It'll be fine. Come on!'

She led the way back out into the hall, checking to either side as Nayland followed her.

'All clear.' She ran to the head of the stairs and waved Nayland along behind her.

'Open the front door,' he whispered. 'Quickly.'

She drew back the bolts and swung the door open. He ran right past her, immediately cutting right and then ducking as he saw Patience appear at the window beside him. He fell back against the wall as Elizabeth joined him, both of them moving low beneath the sill.

'It is ridiculous,' said Elizabeth, 'hiding from your own staff, not free to do what you like in your own home.'

'It hasn't stopped you in the past.'

'Just get to the garage.'

They ran together, moving around the side of the house to an outhouse that had been designed to look like a stable. In fact, it housed two or three cars and a motorcycle that Nayland had fallen in love with but had never mastered riding.

'The keys!' said Nayland.

'I didn't even know it was locked.'

'That's because you always get Gerry to drive you everywhere.' Their sullen driver was only too used to his mistress's demands and had actually threatened to leave their employ several times due to her frequent abuse. Nayland had always assumed she had taken such a dislike to him because she had been unable to lure him into her bed.

'So what do we do now?' Elizabeth asked.

'You wait here with her and I go and get them.'

'I'm not sitting out here with the body! What if someone comes along?'

'Charm them. The last thing we need is Patience seeing what you look like. We'll cross that bridge when we come to it. For now let's just deal with this.'

He ran back towards the house, remembering his jacket just as he was about to step through the front door. Why risk it drawing attention? He took it off and threw it to the side of the doorway.

Inside he almost ran right into Patience. 'Sir,' she said, managing to appear only slightly startled, 'I heard someone outside and I wondered . . .'

'We're just heading out.'

'Does Gerry know? I think I saw him sitting in the kitchens.'

'I want to drive – you know I like to drive.'

Patience knew better than to argue, even though he was speaking far too quickly, not acting natural at all.

'Get me the keys, would you?' he asked, trying to decide which car had the biggest trunk. 'The Daimler. I just need to grab something from upstairs.'

'Of course, sir. Might I ask . . .?'

'What?'

'Is the maid with you? Only madam did say . . .'

'Yes, she is. Madness, I know, but you don't argue with Elizabeth.'

Patience felt it safer not to comment on that. 'I'll just get the keys.'

Nayland suddenly panicked. 'Meet me back here, yes?'

Patience gave him a brief look of concern but nodded and walked off towards the kitchens.

Nayland needed to calm down before he aroused any more suspicion. He could probably pass it off as frustration at Elizabeth, anger at her stupid idea to take the maid out. Patience would probably believe that. However much Elizabeth seemed to think that the housekeeper would do as she was told, Nayland knew there was a puritan heart beating away in the woman somewhere. He had no doubt that she wouldn't cover for them if she suspected murder. Some things were beyond her duty.

He ran up the stairs and into Elizabeth's bath-room, wanting to check for any signs of what they had done.

They. It suddenly hit him that, as always, he had made himself part of Elizabeth's business. Something that should have been hers to bear alone was now a weight on his shoulders too.

He grabbed a towel and rubbed at the bath. Elizabeth had done a fair job of cleaning but their wrestling with the corpse had left traces of its own. He ran the towel over the floor, mopping up a couple of blood spills, and then wrapped it up into a tight bundle.

Going back into the dressing room, Nayland grabbed a small holdall, shoved the towel into it and then ran his hands through Elizabeth's clothes until he found what he was after: another red dress, different of course from the other one but close enough. He bundled that into the bag too and ran to his room to fetch another jacket and a tie. He slung the jacket on, folding the tie into his pocket, and ran back downstairs.

'The keys, sir.' Patience held them out to Nayland and he grabbed them without replying.

Having second thoughts at the door he turned back to her. 'Knowing Elizabeth it will be a long night,' he said. 'Don't worry about waiting up – we'll manage.'

'Very good, sir.' Patience showed no sign of being pleased about the early night but Nayland hadn't expected her to. He'd seen her smile just twice while she'd been working for them, both times under extreme duress.

He tried to look casual as he left the house, pulling the door closed gently behind him before grabbing his bloodstained jacket from the ground, stuffing it into the bag and breaking into a run.

'What took you so long?' Elizabeth asked, still waiting in the shadows behind the garage.

'Trying to cover our tracks,' he said, handing her

the bag and the car keys. 'The Daimler, that's the big black one . . .'

'I know, I know . . .'

'Open the trunk.'

Nayland picked up Georgina's body and followed on behind Elizabeth, keeping a lookout over his shoulder in case anyone was watching from the house.

Elizabeth fussed with the keys and finally opened the trunk. Nayland dropped the body into it, slamming the metal lid down with relief. It was good not to have to look into those eyes for a while.

'What's in the bag?' Elizabeth asked.

'A bloodstained towel, my jacket and another red dress.'

'What do we need another red dress for?'

'So we can be seen.'

They drove in silence. Elizabeth lost in her own thoughts, Nayland too terrified to intrude on them. He pulled over at a call box once they hit the Boulevard.

'I want to speak to Marie,' he said once the call was answered.

'Who's speaking?'

'Someone who knows better than to give his name to a guy he doesn't know. Just put her on, for Christ's sake.'

There was a couple of minutes' pause and then

Nayland's right ear was filled with a French accent that sounded as if it had been fried in tobacco and vodka. 'Who is it?' Marie asked.

'Nayland. I want company for the evening.'

'But of course you do, darling. Who doesn't? Anyone in particular?'

'Is Val free?'

'For you? Everybody is free, my love. Do you want me to have her drop by?'

'No, I'll come to you.'

'A personal visit? How thrilling. When?'

'Soon. Maybe half an hour.'

'Oh sweetness, you're not giving me much time to make the best of myself.'

'Like you need it.'

'God but I love you, darling man. Come quickly so I can kiss you!'

She hung up.

Marie had never been to France in her life, though she had spent one passionate night in Paris, Texas during her distant youth. Even now she looked back fondly on her 'Lovely Cowboy' and the hours they had spent in a flophouse by the rail tracks. 'I came more often than the fast train to Houston,' she would joke to anyone who would listen.

The accent matched the heavy red and black satin she often wore and she felt it conferred a sense of class on what, in all honesty, was a pretty sordid business. For all its moral grey area, however, there wasn't a single business in Los Angeles that wouldn't have killed for Marie's client list. There were few famous names from either side of the camera lens that hadn't used her services at some point during their careers. She was terrifyingly expensive and there was nothing the movie industry approved of more than an unwieldy invoice. It spoke of value, exclusivity and discretion.

The business was run out of a small hotel just off Franklin Avenue. It had the look of an old Cajun residence, a slice of Southern decadence in the heart of the city, and was surrounded on all sides by a high wall that kept the inquisitive at bay.

Nayland pulled up further along the street, not wanting to be so brazen as to park right outside the front gates.

Elizabeth pulled on the door handle but Nayland leaned over and shut the door.

'I'm not sure that's a good idea.'

'Why the hell not?'

'Because of the way you look . . . Jesus, Elizabeth, people are going to be asking questions.'

'Then let them. I haven't done this to hide it, I want people to see. What's the point otherwise?'

Nayland sighed and nodded. It was obvious she wasn't going to hide the effect of her bloodletting: as far as she was concerned you didn't paint a beautiful picture and then hide it in the attic. He would just have to hope that they could weather the inevitable storm of media curiosity that her appearance would cause.

They walked to the front gates and Nayland rang the bell. He looked around, unhappy to be loitering outside what, for all its glamorous reputation, was still a whorehouse.

'Good evening, sir and madam,' came a deep voice from between the bars.

There was the creak of old iron and then they were standing inside. The doorman, a towering black man whose muscular body stretched every stitch of his old-fashioned footman's uniform, looked like a relic from the seventeenth century, Nayland thought. He played the part beautifully, stockinged calves turned out as he bowed and gestured for Nayland and Elizabeth to walk ahead of him up the drive. The front courtyard was filled with the whisper of fountains, shedding cut-glass crystal reflections of the moon into a deep pool that could have contained all manner of creatures beneath its fat lily pads.

'It's lovely,' said Elizabeth, eyeing the servant with unabashed hunger.

'Indeed, madam,' he replied, showing no sign of being aware of her appreciation. 'My mistress likes to surround herself with beautiful things.'

'Indeed she does,' Elizabeth replied, touching the man gently on his arm.

Nayland couldn't hide his irritation at her open flirting. Everything he was doing for her and the first chance she got she was fluttering her damned eyelashes at niggers. The woman made his blood boil.

'Come on,' he said, tugging her towards the door. 'Leave the slaves alone.'

'Slaves?' Elizabeth laughed and looked towards the doorman. 'You'll have to forgive my husband, darling. He's such a racist pig.'

The doorman smiled and waved the comment away. 'I *am* a slave, though not in the way that sir suggests. My mistress makes it quite clear that my body is not my own.'

Elizabeth roared with laughter at that. 'How wonderful! I love Marie more and more by the moment.'

Nayland bit his tongue as the doorman loomed past him, opening the door for them.

The inside of the house was as decadent as its exterior. Black and white floor tiles, heavy red drapes, dark wood. Everything chosen for its opulence.

'If you would please follow me through to the right.' The doorman led the way, pushing a heavy pair of double doors open to reveal a spacious parlour whose colour scheme was every bit as deep and rich as that of the entrance hall.

'My darlings!' Marie was reclining on a

chaise longue, wrapped in a confection of black lace and red satin, her considerable bulk glistening in the light of countless candles. 'How fabulous to have you here.'

She got to her feet, gave Nayland a lingering kiss on each cheek and then turned to Elizabeth. The pause was surprisingly brief but no less marked for it. 'Oh Elizabeth, darling,' she said, 'what have you done? I swear you look younger than ever.' Marie held Elizabeth's hands. 'You simply must give me the secret, it's . . .' She turned Elizabeth from side to side, inspecting her from all angles. 'It's breathtaking. I hate you with a passion.' She pulled her close. 'You have to give me his name, darling, anyone that can achieve what I see before me . . . I've heard how these doctors are getting better every day but I never imagined how good they were.' She suddenly realised that her appreciation could also be seen as criticism. 'Not that you weren't stunning enough to begin with, naturally.'

'I owe it all to the most fabulous new treatment from India,' said Elizabeth. 'I can't remember the last time I ate a solid meal but it's worth every sacrificed mouthful.'

'Oh, I am a slave to the sweet.' Marie sat back down and gestured for Elizabeth and Nayland to follow suit. 'I just can't stop filling my mouth, can I, Robert?'

'Indeed not, mistress,' the doorman replied, not

acknowledging the double entendre but bowing low towards her. 'Can I provide anything else?'

Marie looked to Nayland and Elizabeth. 'We won't be staying, I'm afraid,' said Nayland. 'We have a table booked at Gabrizzi's.'

'Oh Lord, I think half of me is made from their peppered escalope,' said Marie, waving Robert away. 'The lovely Benito sometimes delivers for me as these days I rarely leave the house.'

'You must get lonely,' said Elizabeth.

'Not a bit of it, nor do I get bored. I have everything and everyone I need within these four walls. In fact, the only time I do leave is to get a little peace and quiet.'

'Well, I can't promise that,' Elizabeth replied, 'but we'll be having a party at the end of the month and I would adore it if you could come.'

'Perhaps bring a few of my friends?'

'Absolutely.'

'Oh, I'm sure that would be utterly divine – it's been years since you last had one of your gatherings. About time that lovely garden of yours was put to good use again, I'm sure it does the bougainvillea no end of good. Mine positively explodes all over the place.'

'Is Val ready?' Nayland asked, eager to be moving again, only too aware that they were still driving around with a dead body in the trunk. He wouldn't relax until that was safely dumped somewhere the coyotes would find it.

'Such an eager boy,' Marie smiled at him. 'If only Elizabeth would let me borrow you for a night – I'd love to see that energy at work.'

'Help yourself,' Elizabeth laughed. 'We're not restrictive in our marriage, are we, darling?'

Nayland couldn't think of a polite reply to that. Marie, perhaps sensing his discomfort, filled the silence. 'She's ready and waiting,' she said, standing up and tugging at a heavily tasselled bell rope. 'Will you be bringing her home or shall I have Robert come and collect her?'

'We'll bring her back,' Nayland assured her.

'In one piece or not, I leave it up to you. Val's a resilient little thing.'

The door opened and the girl herself walked in. She was, as Nayland remembered, perfect for his plans. About the same height and build as Georgina (though with considerably better bearing), she would fulfil her role admirably.

'Oh, she'll be in one piece, all right,' Nayland assured Marie. 'We just want to take her out for the night.'

Back in the car, Nayland pulled the red dress from the bag and handed it to Val on the back seat. She gazed at it somewhat dreamily. He was quite sure she was doped: she certainly moved like a woman whose feet weren't quite touching the ground.

'We'd like you to wear this,' he said.

'Whatever you like,' Val said, leaning back against the upholstery and unfastening the black dress she had been wearing. 'Do you want to watch?'

'That's fine,' he said, though he couldn't quite manage to keep his gaze from the rear-view mirror as she writhed in the limited space.

'So,' he said to his wife, 'where do you want to go?'

'Anywhere there will be cameras!'

They spread themselves wide.

First they gatecrashed Gabrizzi's. Nayland was concerned that neither of them had the reputation to sidestep the reservation list but Elizabeth's beauty weaved its magic. It was an exercise in nostalgia, watching how easily a pretty face opened doors. Nayland remembered how it had been when they had first broken out in this town, surrounded by eagerness, curiosity, adoration and the flash of cameras. Nothing had been out of their reach, everyone, everywhere wanting to brush up against them in the hope that something would rub off.

Now the city was at it again. This time none of it was for him, it was all about Elizabeth. Of all the emotions he had anticipated feeling as a result of what she had done, jealousy had been the last thing he'd expected. He had to admit it was tempered with a degree of admiration: watching her work the crowds was to witness an astonishing thing. She bounced from one group to another, each shocked by her incredible transformation.

'It's all about mung beans,' she told one. 'A serum from China,' she told another. 'Exercise and meditation,' yet another.

Everywhere she went the explanation was met with the same responses: a knowing smile, a pretence to have heard of the power of such curatives, a claim to be considering doing just the same.

I live in a city of idiots, Nayland thought, *or is it just that we've been making up dreams and fantasies for so long that we'll believe anything?* He supposed that was the real answer: the terrible act she had committed to forge her new beauty was no less absurd than any of her excuses. Who could have thought that bathing in the blood of the young would have any effect at all beyond impending insanity and a prison sentence? Ultimately they couldn't dispute the evidence. Elizabeth looked half her age, and most of them only cared about the how of it so they could do it themselves. In a world of image she was once again the queen.

From Gabrizzi's they went to the Tip-Top Club, where Elizabeth continued to hold court, moving between the tables as if she owned the place. Nayland sat still, drinking the bar dry while Val watched.

'You want to go outside?' she asked him.

'Just drink your drink,' he replied, unable to take his eyes off his wife.

Val shrugged and did as she was told. If he wanted to pay her to get drunk then that was fine by her.

From there they went to the Hot Shoe Lounge and that was where Nayland eventually lost track of Elizabeth altogether. One minute she had been carving up the dance floor, the next she was gone, leaving Nayland stranded in the club with Val on his arm and a dead body in the trunk of his car.

He realised that this didn't surprise him one bit as he stared into the bottom of his glass and fed on the dregs.

Elizabeth was on fire. She felt like a starving man at a banquet, gorging herself on the adoration and attention that she had missed for so many years.

As she had predicted, the response to her new appearance had been jealousy rather than incredu - lity. She laughed to see the poisonous looks from her contemporaries (hell, her descendants!) and basked in the hungry stares she got from the men on their arms. You only realise what power is when you've been without it. She relished that power.

Perhaps, perversely, that was what first attracted her to Henry.

Not that he wasn't handsome – he was,

aggressively so. He was also immaculate, from the cut of his suit that alternately hugged and hung from him – an extension of his body, not just something that covered it – to the thin moustache that drew a line above his soft yet powerful mouth. He was young (and now so was she) and he didn't look at her like the other men. Most of the boys in the room had an open hunger on their faces, a desire that was unmistakable. Henry simply looked amused. He was interested, yes, he made eye contact, he laughed at Elizabeth's jokes, he listened to her talk, but he talked back, he told her about himself, assuming her interest in him. When they danced they moved apart as much as they moved together. He swung his hips with a sexual confidence that she recognised in herself. He knew he was exciting, he knew he was sexy, he knew that she was as lucky to be talking to him as he was to her. Quite simply he was the most attractive man in the room, knew it and worked it. He was her. And if that wasn't a decent challenge then what was?

Elizabeth kept an eye on Nayland, turning his whiskies sour with the intensity of his disapproving expression. He wanted her for himself, of course he did – hadn't she encouraged as much in him from the very first day they had met? But she had fought that battle and won; there was simply no pleasure in fighting it again.

'Let's go somewhere else,' she had suggested to

Henry, whispering into his ear as they danced. 'Let's just vanish and leave them all with nothing to look at.'

He had smiled, nodded and then, on the key change, swung her from the floor and out through the backstage.

They left the atmosphere of smoke and music that sizzled in the air like caramelised sugar. In the open air a cool breeze was coming in from the coast and Elizabeth felt clean and new as she ran with Henry down the street.

They grabbed a taxi, jumping into the back, laughing at the perfection of their escape.

'Where to now?' he asked.

'Your place,' she said, 'not mine. I'm tired of dancing in company.'

He nodded and told the driver to head to the Hollywood Hotel.

She couldn't have been more pleased. Of course that was where he was staying, was there anywhere more perfect? Anywhere more entrenched in the bedrock of this place?

It had seen better years, certainly. It had been built as the new century was born, opening its doors in 1902 and looking out over what would one day become Hollywood Boulevard. Since then it had been a hive of glitterati, everyone from Carl Laemmle to Rudolph Valentino having stayed under its roof.

When she had first arrived in Hollywood, Elizabeth had spent some time there, regularly attending the dances, smiling at the great and good who surrounded her, making her mark, turning heads. Entering now, she did her best to be invisible, something she was sure she had never done before.

They ran up the stairs to Henry's room, managing to avoid all but the briefest glances from the staff (who knew their job well enough to turn a blind eye). Once inside, Elizabeth relaxed and stopped trying to hide herself. In fact she did the opposite, showing Henry everything he had a wish to see. Once they had feasted on each other enough, they lay back on the bed and talked.

'You're married?' he asked.

This confused her for a moment because she was so used to people knowing who she was. 'Yes, for business reasons.'

'There are business reasons for marriage?'

'You haven't been in the business long, have you?'

'I'm not really in it at all yet. I just met a guy who seems to think I have a chance of doing well here. To be honest, I've never been that into movies.'

'You met a guy . . .?'

'Yeah, I know how it sounds but he seems on the level. He's paying for me to stay here, shipping me around the studios, getting me meetings.'

'Watch your back. I give it a week before someone's put a knife in it.'

'I'm capable of looking after myself. What about you? You're an actress?'

Coming from anyone else Elizabeth would have taken this as an insult. Even then, happy for the first time in years, she had to bite back the urge to slap him.

'Yes,' she replied, as evenly as she could, 'I'm an actress.'

'Sorry.' He smiled. 'Don't feel insulted that I don't recognise you. Like I said, I don't know jack about movies. I've been crushing egos all night long with my ignorance.'

'It doesn't matter,' she said and surprised herself by almost meaning it: sincerity was an unusual experience. 'It's good to get outside all that once in a while.'

'Yeah, I guess it must be hard. Everyone knowing everything about you.'

'It's not that. Nobody knows a thing – it's all stories, on the screen and off it. It's the expectation, the awareness, the fact that you can't surprise anybody any more. You become part of the establishment.'

'You can't have been working long.'

'Longer than you think, and that's the problem. I realised tonight how wonderful it is at the begin - ning, when you're climbing, when nobody quite knows what to expect from you. Enjoy it while it lasts, the plateau is boring.'

'You seem confident that I'll make it, then?'

'Oh, of course you'll make it. Hollywood will always love pretty.'

Nayland stumbled out into fresh air a few hours later, the ever-reliable Val on his arm.

'Where did your wife go?' she wanted to know. She wasn't the only one, but she was the only one dumb enough to ask.

'Who knows?' he said, shuffling towards the car. 'And who cares?'

'I get it,' she said, with a dope-hazy smile. 'You have that kind of marriage.'

'You don't know the half of it,' he admitted, letting her into the passenger seat and working his way around to the driver's side.

'I think it's healthy,' she said once they were on their way.

'Healthy?'

'Well, people don't stay together in this town,' Val explained. 'I see it all the time, husbands and wives rolling up on Marie's doorstep because they can't bear staying at home. At least you two give each other the freedom to do what you like. It'll make you stronger.'

'What the hell do you know?' Nayland replied. 'There's nothing healthy about our damn marriage.'

'Sorry.' She was well-trained enough to seem genuinely contrite. 'I was just trying to be nice.'

Nayland certainly wasn't used to that sort of behaviour – he had been so starved of politeness that now it irritated him. It was as false as everything else.

'Just be quiet,' he said, 'I don't want to talk about it.'

'That's fine, honey,' she said. 'I'm here to do whatever you want.'

At that moment all he wanted to do was drive. He worked his way around the streets, aimless and frustrated, taking out his anger between stop signs as he revved the engine and forced the car to move faster and faster along the almost empty streets. He could tell that Val was getting nervous next to him: no doubt she'd seen her fair share of violent clients and was wondering if she'd found another. He liked that, deciding that sometimes the only pleasure left for a man who suffers cruelty is to visit it on others. He watched her out of the corner of his eye as she dug her nails into the car upholstery, terrified that he was going to lose control and send them crashing into something.

'I know you're angry,' she said eventually, putting her hand on his leg, 'but sooner or later you're either going to kill us both or have the cops chasing us.'

It was the latter thought that brought Nayland to

his senses. If the police pulled him over and checked his trunk they would be asking about a lot more than reckless driving. Reluctantly he slowed his speed, clenching the steering wheel all the tighter as he headed out of the city.

'Where are we going?' Val asked him as they left the city behind, driving up into the hills and dark skies uncluttered by neon and street lights.

'I just need to breathe,' Nayland said, cutting onto Mulholland and out towards the parkland and the canyons.

'We all need that, baby,' she agreed, 'to rise up out of the city and taste what the world was like before we broke it.'

'You're pretty philosophical for a hooker.'

'Perfect job for it. We spend most of our time on our backs thinking about something else.'

He'd asked for that. She stroked his thigh nonetheless, realising she shouldn't upset her client any more than he already was. 'Not that I'd be like that with you.'

'Yeah, you would,' he said, 'and me with you. We'd both be thinking of other bodies, other souls.'

Val had more sense than to ask Nayland who he would be thinking about. She just carried on stroking his leg as he drove through the trees, lifting them up and up above the city.

'What do you take?' he asked her after a few minutes of silence.

'What do you mean?'

'You know what I mean. You've been hopped up all night.'

'It helps sometimes.'

'I'm sure. What is it?'

Val opened her purse, pulling out a small leather case containing a hypodermic syringe. 'Heroin. Everyone injects it these days, it's not a problem. Want to try it?'

'No.' Nayland hadn't been asking just out of curiosity. 'But I don't mind if you do.' He held out his hand. 'But not just yet. I want you clear-headed for a little longer.'

She fixed him with a lopsided smile. It had all the charm of a makeshift banner erected outside a building site. 'The night is young, huh?'

'Younger than me.'

He hadn't been fishing for compliments and she sensed as much, deciding that he didn't expect or want a reply.

Nayland pulled off the road, parking in a perfect vantage point above the lights and coursing veins of the city's highways.

'Time to breathe?' Val asked.

He nodded and got out, moving to look at the view. He glanced down, pleased to note how the land fell away beneath them and rolled down through bushes and vines into a valley inhabited only by wildlife and trees. Perfect.

'One day I think I'd like to move out up here,' said Val, looking over his shoulder. 'I'm a country girl at heart. I like wide-open spaces. I like to see the stars.'

A more arrogant actor might have told her she was looking at one right now but Nayland stayed silent. He just led her back to the car and took off that damned red dress he had made her wear.

Looking at her laid back on the warm bonnet of the car, a piece of lean barbecue on the skillet, he luxuriated in how different she was from Elizabeth. Where his wife was curved, Val was slender, a quiet body as opposed to the loudspeaker yell of voluptuousness that Hollywood had fallen in love with.

She reached out to Nayland, a reasonable pretence of lust to which he had the good grace to respond. Stripping off and savouring the feel of the breeze on a body he had no cause to be shy about in such undemanding company.

He made love to her, a change from the physical combat of sex with Elizabeth, and did his best to put himself in the moment, to get out of his head and take the time to be with this woman, on this hill, on this night. He was not so self-deluded as to imagine she might do the same.

When they'd finished he lay next to her while they smoked cigarettes and looked up at the stars she was so enamoured of. He realised he could no longer remember the names of any of them.

'Now you can take your drug,' he said. 'Float away to wherever it is that you go and I'll drive you home.'

He was slightly saddened at the speed with which she slid off the bonnet, eager for her fix.

Val picked up the red dress but he shook his head. 'You don't have to wear that any more. Put your own dress back on.'

She shrugged, reached into the passenger seat for her purse and then climbed into the back seat. Nayland smoked another cigarette, listening out for the sounds of her cooking up, the smell of toasting opiate filtering out of the window. He gave it another couple of minutes, then walked around to the back door and looked through the window. Val was lying there, eyes closed, drifting away to the only truly open space that she could find these days. Satisfied that she was out of it and no threat as a reliable witness, he opened the trunk, picked up Georgina and quickly threw her off the edge of the ravine. She tumbled away into darkness but he heard her continue to roll, snapping branches and crunching undergrowth for a good few seconds after he lost sight of her.

Nayland closed the trunk, got dressed and sat on the fender for a few more minutes to smoke yet another cigarette. He was in no rush to go home. He was in no rush to return to a life that offered nothing. How wonderful would it be just to keep driving? Val could stick around; they could drive down the coast, find somewhere quiet to kick back and just be.

He sighed. It sounded like the plot of a movie and that was one thing his life would never be. Nobody would film such a shambolic descent into self-pity.

He threw his cigarette stub into the canyon after the body of the maid and his last real chance of making good on a thoroughly wasted life.

Elizabeth woke up with her skin burning.

The awareness crept into her consciousness swiftly so that by the time her eyes were open she was gritting her teeth with the pain.

Next to her, Henry was snoring loudly so she rolled out of bed as carefully as she could and ran into the bathroom. What she saw in the mirror nearly forced a scream out of her despite her attempts to stay quiet. Her youthful looks were gone, replaced with a face even older than she had possessed before. Only by a few years, perhaps: the odd extra line here and there, an extra puffiness beneath the eyes.

Slowly the pain on her skin faded away, leaving one that reached altogether deeper.

She got dressed and ran, terrified and dejected, for home.

SECOND REEL: THE BRIGHTEST STAR

NEWSPAPER HEADLINES SPIN TOWARDS THE SCREEN, THE FAST SPIRALS HALTING AS THEY PRESENT THEMSELVES ON A DIAGONAL. THERE IS A FANFARE OF THE BRASS SECTION:

'THE QUEEN OF HOLLYWOOD RETURNS' shouts one.

'BEAUTY AT THE BALLROOM' cries another.

'GLITZ AND GLAMOUR AT GABRIZZI'S' announces a third.

PHOTOS COME THICK AND FAST TO ACCOMPANY THE HEADLINES. IN EVERY SINGLE ONE OF THEM ELIZABETH CAN BE SEEN TO SPARKLE EVEN THROUGH THE GRAINY NEWSPRINT. SHE IS BACK AND THE WORLD HAS NOTICED.

Henry woke to second-hand sunshine glinting off the mirror at the foot of his bed and shining right in his face. With a growl he got out of bed and yanked the curtain half closed to cut off the beam. Then he noticed he was alone.

'Stood up?' he mumbled.

He wouldn't normally have minded. After all, it had been no more than a bit of fun following a night of drinking and dancing – hadn't he sneaked away with the dawn after a few of those in his time? Still, he had liked Elizabeth, and for more than just her beauty. There had been a sadness to her, an old wisdom that had made her seem both weary and yet determined. In a world where the beauty he was introduced to gave clear signs of there being nothing beneath the surface it had made a refreshing change. He had been determined to dig a little, see what he might find.

The phone rang.

'Henry, my boy!' shouted his manager, as if he was stumbling upon his protégé in a crowded room rather than calling him direct on the phone. 'I hear you were painting the town red last night?'

'I went out,' Henry admitted. 'That OK?'

'Hell, yes! We want people talking about you. Go out, dance the night away and end up in bed with the most beautiful woman you can find. If she's famous all the better.'

'Well . . . now you come to mention it . . .'

'That's my boy! Listen, hold that thought – you can tell me all about it at breakfast. You eaten?'

'No.'

'Neither have I and it's driving me wild. What's the point in mornings unless you fill them with breakfasts? I'll pick you up in half an hour.'

Henry decided to wait out front. He was happy to get out of a room that was stale with old cigarette smoke and sex. It felt as though his hangover had infected the furnishings.

Outside there was a strong Hollywood sun and a breeze that was taking the edge off the heat. A world away from the dull skies that used to loom over his old life in New York. Here you looked up and wondered if you were seeing eternity. These were the kind of skies you dreamed of flying in.

The car pulled up and Fabio opened the door. 'What the hell you doing out here? They kick you out?'

'Just getting some air.'

'That stuff's bad for you. Let's drench it in maple syrup.'

They drove to a little cafe that Fabio claimed 'served the best damned eggs in town'. (Though Henry was at a loss as to how an egg could be that varied – surely it was either cooked or it wasn't?)

They took a table near the window. 'You don't get anywhere in this town by hiding,' said Fabio.

'Let them walk past and see the next brightest star that's going to light up the screen.'

'Anyone offered anything?' Henry asked, because to him you could only be a star if you'd appeared in a film.

'Give it time, I'm not even considering offers just yet. We want people to wonder if they can even get you. Leave them hanging, let them panic that the other studio sent a better script, offered a bigger package.'

Henry shrugged. Fabio seemed to know what he was doing and he was paying, so let him play it however he wanted to.

'I'll have the steak and eggs,' Henry told the waitress. 'Keep cooking the steak until the chef cries.'

'Philistine,' said Fabio, before ordering eggs benedict with blueberry pancakes to follow.

'Two breakfasts?' Henry asked with a smile.

'Pancakes are dessert – why shouldn't breakfast come with dessert? Every other damn meal does.'

He got up and walked over to a newspaper stand next to the food counter, grabbed a copy of the daily *Variety* and brought it back to the table. 'Am I going to find you in this?' he asked, 'I damn well hope so . . . "Bright young thing lights up—"'

He stopped speaking, a rare event in itself, struck by the front page.

Henry glanced over. 'That's Elizabeth, the girl I was with last night.'

Fabio couldn't tear his eyes away from the picture. 'But it can't be . . .' he muttered.

The waitress arrived with their coffee and had to work around what appeared to be a statue of a fat man holding a newspaper. Fabio gave no indication that he even saw her.

'You know her?' Henry asked eventually, feeling someone had to get the conversation moving again.

'Know her?' Fabio finally put the paper down, though he still didn't take his eyes off the photo. 'She's another one of my clients.'

'Is that incest?' Henry joked.

Fabio looked at him. 'You shitting me?' he asked. 'You actually slept with her?'

'Well . . .' Henry suddenly realised that maybe he had spoken out of turn. He tried to think of a way he could retract what he had already said. There was little point in doing so.

'Oh Jesus . . .' sighed Fabio, 'you slept with Elizabeth.'

'She did say she was married,' Henry admitted, 'but that it was a business thing . . .'

'Then maybe both of you need lessons in how to keep your goddamn mouths shut. What am I working my ass off for here if everyone's going to run around contradicting my careful work?'

'Sorry . . .'

'Don't apologise, I'm just amazed you got out

with your dick still attached. I mean, Elizabeth . . . she's a piece of work.'

Henry assumed Fabio was paying Elizabeth a compliment and smiled. 'She certainly is – the most beautiful woman in the room and she knew it.'

'The most . . .' Fabio pulled the paper closer and scrutinised the grainy black and white picture intently. 'How old would you say Elizabeth is?'

Henry shrugged. 'Older than she looks, I guess. I know she's been in the business a little while. Maybe twenty-five?'

Fabio stared at him for a moment, then returned to the picture in the newspaper. He didn't think Henry was bullshitting him: he wasn't the sort of kid who would lie about that sort of thing. He called a spade a damned spade.

Fabio put the newspaper down. 'We need to wrap this up quick. I think I should pay Elizabeth a visit.'

'Have I done something wrong?'

'Probably not. Or if you have it's nothing that countless other guys in this town haven't done over the years.'

Henry took that to be a general point rather than a reference to Elizabeth in particular, thereby misunderstanding Fabio completely. Which was probably for the best: while the young man didn't know Elizabeth well he was old-fashioned enough to the point where he would have tried to defend

her honour, whether she actually possessed any or
not.

The waitress arrived with their breakfast. Fabio's
sense of urgency wasn't strong enough to stop him
eating it.

Filled with carbohydrates and caffeine, Fabio had
his driver take him to Elizabeth and Nayland's
house. As if his mood wasn't unsettled enough
already he met the police in the driveway.

'What the hell are they doing here?' he asked
nobody in particular. 'Jesus . . . are these two trying
to give me a heart attack?'

The fact that he was doing a good enough job of
that on his own escaped him, naturally, and he
lit a cigar as the car pulled up outside the front
door.

The driver rushed around to release both him
and the clouds of smoke he was producing and he
stepped out onto the gravel just as the police car
drove away.

'Police, Nayland?' he shouted. His client was
standing in the open doorway. 'Please tell me it's
nothing to worry about.'

'It isn't,' Nayland replied. 'One of the staff has
gone missing, that's all.'

'One of the staff? What the hell has that got to do
with you?'

'Nothing, but I've had to work hard to reassure

the police of that fact. It was Georgina Woolrich, one of the maids. We took her out last night and she never went home.'

'You took her out? What are you talking about, you took her out?'

Nayland led Fabio into the house. 'There was an accident. Elizabeth was hurling glassware around the place and the maid got in the way. Nothing serious but I guess Elizabeth panicked, thinking that the girl would cause trouble. So we gave her a little cash bonus and took her out on the town, by way of an apology.'

'Some apology. There was a time when a maid would be grateful if you hit them – it showed you acknowledged their presence.'

'Those glory days are long past,' said Nayland with heavy sarcasm.

'Breaks your heart, don't it? So what's the problem? You took her out . . .?'

'And I thought I'd dropped her off at home but it turns out she gave me the wrong address. The police think she might have been embarrassed for us to see where she really lived.'

'So the dumb kid walks home and something happens to her?'

Nayland shrugged. 'Maybe she'll turn up later, I don't know. Maybe she went on somewhere else. A friend's house or something.'

'Who knows? Whatever, it's not your problem

and if the cops call again you tell me and I'll set them straight on that.'

Fabio walked out onto the patio. 'Get whatever staff you have left to rustle up some coffee, would you? I want to talk with you both.'

'Both? Elizabeth isn't well, she won't be coming down.'

'The hell she won't. I want to see her for myself.'

'See her?' Nayland had known this moment was coming, of course, but he was damned if he was going to give in to it easily.

Fabio pulled the copy of *Variety* from his jacket pocket and threw it onto the table. 'She's all over the papers. Your night out caused quite a fuss.'

'Isn't that good?'

'Good? It's great. But I don't understand it.' Fabio prodded at the picture on the front page with his finger, as fat and stubby as the cigar he was smoking. 'How is she looking like that only hours after I last saw her?'

Nayland sighed and made a show of looking at the picture. 'She's trying a new regime,' he said. 'Takes years off her – that and favourable lighting has done her the world of good.'

'A new regime? What regime?'

'I don't know, Fabio, she'll tell you all about it when you see her. But not today.'

'I may be lots of things, Frank, but I'm not an idiot. Elizabeth is seen wandering around the town's hottest nightspots and she looks half her age. That may wash with the idiots out there, especially the ones that haven't set eyes on her for five years – which is most of 'em since her career's so far up Shit Creek it's amazing the papers even remember her name – but it doesn't wash with me. I want to know what's going on and I want to know now.'

Nayland kept his calm. Fabio was nothing he couldn't handle.

He shouted through to Patience, asking her to rustle up some coffee, making Fabio wait for his reply.

Nayland sat down at the table, the very image of quiet calm.

'You can't see Elizabeth,' he insisted, 'but you don't need to. You complain about her not matching your ideal one day, then complain again when she does. Just be happy she's causing a stir in public again.'

'Oh, I am happy, Frank, I'm ecstatic. But I'm also nervous that this is something that's going to bite me on the ass. How did you pull it off? What is it? A lookalike? Jesus . . . I'm your manager – this is the sort of thing you can discuss with me, this is the sort of thing I arrange, for Christ's sake. But if I'm not involved I need to know the trick or I'm not going to rest easy.'

'No trick. It's just a cream that she's using, you

know what these women are like. Anyway, the image exaggerates. Like I said, it was good lighting, there's nothing miraculous about it. If you saw her you wouldn't think she looked any different.'

'So let me see her!'

'I told you, not now, she's in bed.'

Fabio raised his arms in despair. 'I can't work like this. I've a good mind to drop you from my client list.'

This was a step-up from his usual threats and Nayland knew it. Still, he refused to rise to the bait.

'That would be a shame. But it's up to you, of course.'

Fabio met Nayland's stare: a momentary game of poker, of bluff and counter-bluff. Fabio was surprised at Nayland's fortitude – the man was normally a pushover. But there was time to turn the tables yet. A good player knew when to fold and when to play on.

He smiled. 'Look at us! How long have we been working together?'

'A good few years.'

'A good few years. And we're going to throw that away over something as stupid as this?'

'Your call.'

'Well, then, one of us needs to be the grown-up and I guess it can be me. But I still want to see Elizabeth. I want to see for myself how good she looks and then make sure we all make the money we deserve.' The coffee arrived and Fabio made complimentary noises, showering Patience with a charm she neither needed or liked. 'This is what I'm talking about,' said Fabio. 'You ask for what you want and it's with you in moments, am I right? The perfect relationship.'

'For the one doing the asking,' Nayland replied.

'That's the world, Frank, it's divided between people that ask and people that do. And we want to stay on the right side of that equation, right?'

Nayland couldn't say he was completely comfortable with this simplistic view but he shrugged and nodded anyway.

'So help me out. If Elizabeth has found some kind of miracle anti-ageing cure and is ready to hit the tiles and turn heads then I need to be working with you on that. I need to turn that into money. Because you need money, Frank – you can't live off memories and this place must be eating up the savings you had.'

Nayland refused to comment on that. He had no doubt that Fabio knew all he needed to know about his client's finances but he, Nayland, was still too English to discuss them openly. Besides, Fabio was right: they were by no means as rich as they had once been. But he had stayed ahead of this game so far and wasn't about to concede a point now.

'It must be,' Fabio continued. 'You need more work. You need bigger successes.'

'You were offering me a movie yesterday.'

'Some crappy horror picture? That's what you want?'

'Yesterday it was a great opportunity.'

'To hell with yesterday, yesterday is gone. Today we should be looking for something bigger. You haven't had press coverage like this for years. My phone will be ringing. So is this a one-off or the start of something?'

Nayland couldn't answer that question. It had been the only thing on his mind all morning. Fabio didn't wait for a reply.

'Because we could be looking at an opportunity here. We could be looking at a route back to the top. If this is more than a lucky break, a moment of good fortune with a drunk photographer in a dark club. If she can make this kind of spread again –' he stabbed at the paper with his finger once more, '– then your career just got a new lease of life.'

Having finally disposed of Fabio, Nayland went upstairs in search of Elizabeth.

She was hiding in her room, drapes closed, a dark cave of tobacco smoke, whisky fumes and misery.

'Have they gone?' she asked, buried in the shadows, the bed sheets wrapped around her like a shroud.

'The police? Yes. They weren't happy but I think we'll be all right.'

'Of course we'll be all right. What can they prove?'

Nayland shrugged. 'I think you're overconfident about how untouchable you are.'

'About this? Rubbish. We're royalty in this town and royalty does as it pleases.' She shifted and he caught a glimpse of her face: mascara run from tears, hair a mess. 'But I don't think I'm invulnerable. Not a bit of it. How could I? All the mirrors are only too happy to remind me how fragile I am.'

'At least you had a taste, a night to remember . . .'

'A taste? What use is that to me? All it did was rub my nose in it. And look at me now, I look older than ever, a shadow, a walking corpse.'

'You look fine.' He tried to sound supportive – even after what she had done he couldn't help but try and stand by her. His self-loathing really was at an all-time low. As was his ability to convince her because the words failed to stick.

'I look horrid!' Elizabeth shouted. 'Worse than ever.'

Nayland sat on the edge of the bed. 'It's all over the newspapers,' he said, throwing down the copy of *Variety* that Fabio had left for them. 'Fabio was insufferably excited.'

'Fabio's been here?'

'Just left – did you think it would take him long? He sniffs money.'

Elizabeth pulled the newspaper closer, opened it out and lost herself in the front page. After a moment she began to cry. It took a moment for Nayland to recognise the noise: it had been so long since he had seen her this fragile and exposed. He didn't know quite how to respond.

'I won't have it!' she said. 'Not now, not after last night. I won't go back to this.'

'What choice is there?' he asked, though he knew and dreaded the answer.

'Don't be an idiot,' she replied. 'It worked before and it will work again. I just need more blood.'

'No,' he insisted, trying to sound as firm as he could. 'I helped you last night because the deed was done. Nothing I could do was going to give that girl her life back. But I won't stand by and let you do it again.'

'"Let me"? You're not my keeper. I'll do what I want.'

'And I'll go to the police.'

'What? And go to the chair with me, as an accomplice? Don't think I can't make sure that the blame falls on you, Frank Nayland. I may be old but there's power in these ageing eyelashes yet.' Elizabeth pressed her hands together, the very image of the terrified and repentant woman. 'Oh officer . . . he made me watch while he cut her! I was so terrified but he gets so angry . . . I didn't know what to do! For all I knew it might be me next . . .'

'You fucking bitch.' Nayland had known she was more than capable of this kind of blackmail; in truth there was very little she wasn't capable of, as she had proven last night. But in that moment he hated her more than he had ever imagined he could.

'Damn right I'm a bitch! And I'll do whatever needs to be done for the both of us!'

'Don't drag me into it. This is all about *you*!'

'Really? And I suppose Fabio didn't promise it would help your career too? Don't give me that. It benefits you just as much to be seen with the most beautiful woman in Hollywood.'

'But then I rarely am, am I? You have other gentlemen in mind.'

'Is it that again? Jealousy?'

Nayland wouldn't be so easily sidetracked. 'Dress it up however you want to, but this is about your hunger, your greed . . . I don't come into it.'

'You do if I pull you in, and be assured I will. I need more blood and you're going to help me get it!'

Nayland couldn't remember ever feeling so lost, not only because of where his blind devotion had got him but because he knew where it was going to take him next.

What was he to do? He had no doubt that Elizabeth would be a woman of her word: if it all came to light then she would do her damnedest to push him to the forefront of the whole affair. He could go to the police himself first, of course, get his story in early. Still, there would be no denying his involvement in the disposal of the body. That mess had his hands all over it. Would any jury really believe he had been blameless in the murder itself? Would anyone think he was so weak that he had just come running to do Elizabeth's bidding after the deed was done? Part of him couldn't bear the idea that they could – he was disgusted enough at his own weakness without it being a matter of public record. Even if they did, didn't that still make him an accomplice after the fact? He might just escape the death sentence if he could sell himself as worthless enough. Might. Whatever happened his life as it stood now would be over, he would be sentenced to prison and lose everything. All over the death of a stupid maid.

The only other option was to go with it, to try and make it safe. Women vanished all the time. If they chose more carefully the next time, picked their target with care, maybe they could continue to get away with it. Certainly they would have more chance of success if he was involved in the plan - ning: Elizabeth was a wild card, a madwoman labouring under the impression that she was untouchable by the law. Nayland had no such beliefs. If they slipped up then at best everything would fall down around them, at worst their final performance would be in the electric chair, burning for the pleasure of one last, eager audience.

Nayland wasn't as greedy as Elizabeth but he was just as pragmatic. When it came down to the lives of a few worthless women in exchange for his own – and, yes, an improvement on his own, Fabio had been right about that, he knew that Nayland's star would ascend alongside hers if he let it – well . . . it was a transaction he could accept.

'You're going to do it,' Elizabeth said, her voice no longer angry but quiet and dismissive as if they were discussing nothing more than the purchase of a new suit. 'So let's move on from the recriminations and name-calling and get down to *how* we're going to do it.'

'I hate you sometimes,' Nayland said, not quite willing to let the recriminations lie. 'You're selfish, cruel and evil.'

'I'm also beautiful and the only woman you've ever loved. What does that say about you, darling?' She put her arm around his shoulder and kissed him on the cheek.

'Nothing good,' he admitted, though he couldn't quite bring himself to push her away.

'But with a beautiful wife on your arm the world will be a better place and you know it. You say this is all about me? Fine, think that if you must. But you know deep down that you need the attention as much as I do, the *adoration*.'

This was partly true, though the one person he really needed that adoration from would never provide it.

'We need to be more careful next time,' Nayland said. 'We need to pick someone who won't be so easily missed. Someone who isn't connected with us.'

'In this city? That's easy, the street corners are thronging with them.'

This was certainly true. Marie might cater for Hollywood's exclusive appetites but there were always those further down the rungs of every profession. Could they ask for a better feeding ground?

'People would recognise us.'

'*You*, darling. I don't mind being the butcher but you'll certainly be the man bringing me my animals from market.'

So that was to be the division of labour, was it? Nayland supposed he could live with that.

'Anyway,' Elizabeth continued, 'they don't have to recognise you. Try and remember what it is that you do for a living.'

She had another fair point there. It had been so long since he had done any acting that he had almost forgotten.

'We shouldn't do it here,' he said. 'It adds too many risks.'

'Agreed. We need to find somewhere nearby.

The mountains are covered with old farmhouses and abandoned outbuildings – we must be able to find somewhere.'

'Then get dressed. We'll go and take a look.'

To remember what the area used to be like wasn't difficult once you went off the well-trodden paths. This entire chunk of land had been open fields and farmland before the money and glitter came and carved it all up between them. Still, the abandoned buildings remained, and many of them would stay in good shape until the day when the city's inevitable expansion would swallow them up.

Elizabeth and Nayland found the perfect place only a couple of miles from their house. A small barn surrounded by an orange grove that had been left to grow wild. The long grass was littered with rotting fruit, their cultivator having upped sticks and left once he'd sold enough of his land to let him out of the orange business for good. Nayland imagined he would have packed up his truck and driven away with a smile on his face. Screw long hours in the trees when the idiots from the East Coast had money to burn.

The doors on the barn were intact but unlocked. They could soon see to that – a bit of security was only a length of chain and a padlock away.

Inside was a mess but that could easily be dealt with. The previous owner had abandoned much of his equipment: buckets were piled in the corner and old, rusting tools hung from hooks on the walls.

Nayland looked up. The roof seemed intact, though there was no sure way of telling until it rained.

'It's perfect,' he said.

'It reminds me of home,' Elizabeth replied, not meaning it as a compliment.

'You don't have to live here,' he reminded her. 'It serves one purpose and for that it's ideal.'

He still wouldn't quite meet that 'purpose' head on. While he might have made his decision he was still doing his best to avoid facing its implications.

'Only one way to find out,' Elizabeth said.

'Let's not rush at this.'

'Who's rushing? We've found a place and I want to make myself better again. So find me someone who can help me do that.'

'We still need to get a chain for the door, and somewhere you can actually—'

She pointed behind him. Turning to look he spotted an ancient tin bath, rusted and filled with offcuts of wood.

'You can't use that,' Nayland said. 'It's filthy.' The absurdity of what he was saying suddenly struck him and, on an impulse that seemed to come from nowhere, he burst into laughter.

He supposed it must be shock, an outlet for the

stress he had been feeling over the last twenty-four hours. At least, that was how he tried to convince himself. Better that than admit he was so cold-hearted that he could actually find the situation comic.

Elizabeth had no problem with her own laughter. 'Oh, Frank, you are the silliest idiot sometimes.' She stroked his cheek. 'I know you don't believe it but I do love you a little, you know.'

'A very little.' He got his laughter under control. 'You bloody should do, given what I'm doing for you.'

She reached up and kissed him. 'And don't think I won't thank you again with the body you help me to heal.'

Nayland didn't want even to think about that just yet. But he kissed her back nonetheless, taking his opportunities on the rare occasion they presented themselves.

'Let's get back to the house,' he said. 'I need to get myself ready.'

Nayland was selecting a suitably nondescript outfit from his wardrobe when he noticed the old make-up box. Hidden away behind racks of shoes, it was a buff leather case still filled with the tools of his trade from when he had been working as an actor with touring theatre companies. He remembered the first time he had sat in the make-up studio for a movie, partly thrilled, partly worried that this was a part of the job that was no longer under his control.

He pulled the case out, set it down on the bed and opened it out. Like a doctor's bag it had extendable sections inside that had compartments for his oil sticks, pancake and sponge. There was a lower section containing a couple of bottles of spirit gum, some remover and a selection of false hairpieces. There were also a couple of moustaches and a goatee that had a somewhat piratical air, with the chin-beard working its way to a point. He held the goatee up to his face and looked in the mirror.

'I am Chandu!' he intoned, mimicking the hero of radio and screen. 'Mystic of the magical arts! My power is in my eyes!'

Too much, Nayland decided.

He looked again and found a more conventional beard, this one in light grey.

Looking once more in the mirror he decided it would do the job admirably. He would have to lighten his hair slightly to match (though not as much as he would have liked – it already had a fair amount of grey) but it would go some way towards altering his appearance.

He selected his clothing to match, picking out items that were a little older and more unfashion - able: a sports jacket that was now baggy on him, a plain white shirt and some light grey slacks.

Clothes that wouldn't make an impression. He dressed himself and checked that everything he needed was in the make-up case. One of the bottles of spirit gum had been left slightly open and the contents were now useless but the other was still fine even after years of being ignored.

Nayland was about to leave before a stray thought brought him back to his wardrobe to check the drawers. He pulled out a pair of driving gloves. He'd appeared in enough crime pictures to know that fingerprints were what police nailed criminals on, so why leave any if it could be avoided?

He put the gloves in his pocket and headed out. He checked his watch. He had agreed to meet Elizabeth at the old barn in a couple of hours. She had her own preparations to make.

It was hard to choose a car that was as discreet as his clothes: he had never liked a vehicle that was bland. Settling for the oldest, a Cadillac Le Salle Coupe that at least had been through enough years on the road to have had the edges knocked off it, he headed towards Los Angeles.

As the light began to fade from the sky he pulled over by the side of the road and took a few minutes to fix his make-up. It wasn't perfect, working in such limited conditions, but when you'd fixed your slap in the dressing rooms of places like the inap - propriately named Grand Theatre in Doncaster you could wield an eyeliner anywhere.

By the time he crossed the line into Los Angeles he was in character, hiding as far away from the man who was Frank Nayland as he could. It was better that way, he had decided: let the theatricality of it swallow him whole, all the easier not to feel.

He hadn't been in the city for some months. Hollywood had a habit of forgetting that the outside world existed, becoming its own little bubble community. Besides, for all that he had acclimatised to American life there was still something about its cities that seemed too raucous and alien to Nayland. More and more these days he did his living in his own head, sitting in his viewing room or on the patio with a book. The real world had ceased to offer him much and he gladly avoided its company.

Still, much better that they hunted for prey here than in the incestuous streets so close to home. As the night came alive around him, he was just another cruising driver working his way through the seedy streets looking for a woman.

Nayland had the image of a perfect girl in mind: someone not so attractive, someone who would be glad of the business and not ask too many questions. It took him half an hour before he found her, by which time he had his cover story well prepared.

'Hey honey!' he called. 'You got time for a party?' He had pitched his accent with a New York Bronx flavour. He'd always struggled with American accents, even after all these years, and the more obvious they were the easier.

She was leaning against the closed door of a bakery. No doubt the warm air that sidled up from the vents would keep her warm in the early hours when business got slow and the chill descended. It was hard to guess her age, so thick was the make-up she had applied in order to cover the traces of acne scars. Maybe late twenties, Nayland decided, but pretending to be five years less. Looking at her teeth when she came closer, he saw they were the yellow of a stained toilet pan and as crooked as a drunk's. He decided that she smoked compulsively, probably not just tobacco either.

'What sort of party?' she asked.

'Nothing too major. Two or three friends of mine have rented out a little farmhouse up in the Hollywood Hills and we're all bringing a girl each, you know, to liven things up a bit.'

'Up in the Hills? That's too far.'

'You don't like to travel? It's nice up there. I'll pay you for your time.'

'I'll be gone all night.'

'So I'll pay you for all night. Better for you – no need to be hanging around this place for hours. We'll have a few drinks –' Nayland took a guess, '– plus some dope if you like that kind of thing. Gary's our guy for that, the stuff he gets . . . Jesus, it's like the herb of the gods or something. Anyway,' Nayland just kept talking, acting casual, 'if you don't want to make a night of it then that's up to you. Is there anyone else around here that might feel differently?'

'I like to smoke,' she said, still undecided but clearly wavering.

'Who doesn't? Am I right? Anyway . . . I need to be getting over there before they've nabbed my share, so if you can tell me where I might find someone else I'd be obliged. Hell of a shame, I have to say, honey: you have beautiful hair . . .'

Her eyes lit up even brighter and Nayland felt like a heel. Here he was, trying to lure her with drugs, when all it took to melt her heart was a compliment. 'My mom always said my hair was my best feature.' She ran her fingers through it. It was as yellow and sickly-looking as her teeth.

'Your mom was right.' And where was she now? Nayland wondered. 'Beautiful.' He built in a small pause, a moment in which to reflect. 'But I really got to go.'

'I suppose I could come,' she said, 'as long as you pay the full rate.'

'Money's no problem,' he said. 'What are we talking here? What do you normally earn? Couple of bucks an hour? How about we call it twenty straight? Extra compensation in case you missed a good night.'

The girl sighed. 'Hell, for twenty bucks you can drive me to San Remo, I guess. I got bills and that's the sort of money I can't afford to turn down.'

Nayland reached for his wallet and pulled out the money. 'Let me give it to you up front, that way it's done. I'll drop you home in the morning, too – I've got to head back this way as it is. In fact, I'll throw in breakfast somewhere. I don't know about you but I can eat like a horse the morning after . . .'

She climbed in. 'I don't eat much,' she confessed, then looked awkward as if admitting to some kind of failure. 'But there's nowhere good to eat around here.'

Nayland could believe that – unless you were a rat, at least.

'I get you, the stuff some places serve . . . I think Len was bringing some barbecue so we'll have something to take the edge off the booze when we get there.'

'So, you in town long?' she asked.

'A flying visit, just meeting up with the guys and then heading back east.'

She nodded, well-trained enough not to push it too far with the questions. If a client wanted to talk then they talked: the last thing most of them wanted was the third degree.

Nayland made it easy for her, filling the journey with a fabricated life story, role-play taken to the nth degree. He told the girl about a messy divorce in New York, a woman who had tired of his weeks on the road, selling cleaning products to housewives. He told her how this had been a rebirth, how he now relished his time away, free as a bird, able to go anywhere and do anything. He realised, even as he was speaking, how much of this was wish-fulfilment on his part but once he'd started he found it impossible to stop. Besides, as long as he kept talking she couldn't talk herself and the last thing he wanted was to know anything about her. Let her be two-dimensional. Let her be a cypher. A bit player. If he allowed her to become real he would only feel more guilt.

He kept his eyes on the road, not even wanting to commit her face to memory, and by the time he reached the dirt track for the barn he was in the middle of a nonsensical story about the time he had spent working as a sailor in his youth.

'This the place?' she asked. 'It looks kind of remote.'

'It sure is,' Nayland admitted. 'That's the way we like it. That way we can make all the noise we want and nobody complains.'

As they pulled up outside the barn itself the girl was truly beginning to have doubts. 'There's no sign of anyone else,' she said. 'You sure you got the right place?'

'Sure I'm sure,' he insisted. 'They'll just be inside.'

There was a slight flicker of light coming from

beyond the shuttered windows so she could almost convince herself that he might be telling the truth. She got out of the car, walking just behind him as he headed towards the main door.

'Hey guys!' he shouted. 'Hope you didn't start without us?'

Nayland opened the door and the silence on the other side was a damning answer to his lie.

'I don't like this,' the girl said from behind him. 'What's going on?'

'Honey,' he said, trying his best to make the tone of his voice match the sweetness of the word, 'you worry too much.' He held out his hand and beckoned her to take it. 'What's to be scared of?'

Cautiously, she took his hand. He yanked her violently towards the open doorway and shoved her inside. Pulling the door shut behind her, he leaned against it and tried not to listen as she began to scream.

The door shoved against him as she pushed it desperately, trying to escape, but he held fast. As a solid crunching noise silenced her screams he realised he had been holding his breath. He let it out, gasping in some night air.

'This the best you could do?' came Elizabeth's voice from the other side of the door.

'She's got blood in her,' he said. 'What more do you want? I'll wait in the car.'

'You sure you don't want to watch?' she asked

and he gritted his teeth at the perverse humour in her voice.

'This is your business,' he said. 'I don't want any part of it.'

Nayland walked over to the car, his whole body shaking as the reality of the night's affair crashed in on him and knocked away the foolish games of his constructed persona. A sudden rush of nausea forced him into the shadows beneath the orange trees where he threw up amidst the smell of blossom and warm earth.

He could faintly hear the sound of blood splashing against the inside of the tin bath, like a rainstorm on a corrugated-iron roof. This helped his sickness not one jot and he was trapped there for all of five minutes, dry-heaving under the umbrella of the night sky's beauty.

Once he was sure he could move, he went to lean against the bonnet of the car and fumigate his mouth with a cigarette.

Eventually the barn door opened and Nayland looked up.

Elizabeth was silhouetted against the gas lamps that she had lit inside.

'You finished?' he asked.

She walked forward, escaping the illumination of the lamps and letting the moonlight catch her. She was naked, her skin still streaked with blood. She looked like a freshly born animal.

'How do I look?'

Nayland didn't know what to say. Elizabeth was a nightmare, but one of such sensuality that he found he wanted her anyway. She was a monster, the fruit of her butchery drying in the light night breeze. Beauty daubed with horror.

'You look like you,' he said, truthfully.

'Good,' she replied, lying back in the dust of the ground in front of the barn. 'So come over here and fuck me.'

Later, Nayland helped Elizabeth to store a couple of large clay jars in the far corner of the barn. He knew better than to ask her what they contained. She kept a small bottle to take home.

'I thought it had to be fresh,' he said.

'Who knows? That's what I need to find out. The effect is so short-lived. I need to see how long I can make each body last.'

'Let's hope it works – we can't be picking up a new hooker every day.'

'If only there was someone who could deliver.'

He looked at her, disapproving of her casual joke.

'Don't lecture me again, Frank,' she said. 'I'm not in the mood. Let's just go home, get dressed up and show the world what we're made of.'

And what might that be? he wondered. *Blood and tears and all things evil.*

Nayland kept silent. He was beyond argument now: he had made his bed and the dry earth of it was still smeared across his knees.

They got in the car and he drove them back towards the main road.

Elizabeth rose up in her seat, fishing between her legs. She pulled something out and laughed as she recognised it in the pale light.

'You lost this,' she said, tossing his false beard onto the dashboard. 'When you wear it next you can lick your lips to remind yourself of me.'

Fabio was not quite the liar that most people took him for. He had indeed started his life in Sicily. Like so many in Hollywood he had dragged himself up from simple beginnings: born into a life of penury, the son of a greengrocer and a woman who embroidered with needles as sharp as her tongue. He had been only too eager to see the back of the place and had run away at sixteen for a fresh start in America. While he certainly exaggerated his connections with the world of organised crime, he had served his time in the business during his youth. Running for the Cocozzas, doing odd jobs, making deliveries. He never sank too deep into the life, not through any great sense of morality but rather because he wasn't very good at it. He'd been too small and fat to intimidate anyone (the one time he had been sent to deliver a 'message' to a late-paying client, the man had taken his baseball bat off him and beaten him to a pulp with it). His bosses had been lenient: in fact, they hadn't been in the least bit surprised when he'd come crawling back with loose teeth and a face that looked like a bullet wound. They'd expected it.

'Fabio,' said Giuseppe Avati, a man who would one day fry like overcooked bacon in the electric chair for innumerable counts of murder, 'this just ain't your line of work.'

Which was how Fabio had ended up making his second fresh start. While he was no use at convincing people with his fists, his tongue had considerably more effect and he began to make money working as a salesman. Handling everything from encyclopaedias to stockings, he found that he could charm people and therefore sell to them.

Then, one day, he looked up at the billboards outside the Regent Theater in New York and decided there was a new product on the market, one that he liked very much. The business seemed childishly simple to him: you found someone beautiful and you sold them to the studios, you wrapped them up in a fiction, you told stories, you made audiences fall in love. People were simple and it was no more difficult to press the right buttons in the entertainment industry than it was when you had a suitcase of nylons to shift.

Fabio styled himself as a manager rather than an agent. He worked better with the personal touch and sitting in an office peppering studios with head shots and résumés was not his style. He had gathered a select list of actors over the years, always taking them when they were unknown and then building a story around them, developing them and promoting them until they became something so much bigger than they really were. This had stood him in good stead and he'd always been sharp enough to lift thirty per cent on all the deals he arranged, a high commission but one that he could justify when the actor was suitably hungry for what he had to offer.

The years went by and his childhood in Sicily now seemed a long way away. Still, at heart he was a rural creature, a man of limited origins. However much he played the role of the civilised urbanite that was what he held at his core.

All of which helped to explain why his first response on seeing Elizabeth that night was to cross himself and offer up a prayer to a God whose phone number he had lost many years ago.

Fabio was sitting in the lounge of the Crystal Heart, a new club that had managed to cut itself a slice of the local glitterati's custom and become a hot destination for those looking for fun before midnight. In his opinion, the reputation of the place wouldn't last. Its decor was too contrived and its staff too easily pleased by the sight of a Fairbanks or Pickford taking a table. Treatment of stars was a tricky business: you had to show that you knew who they were but you should never fawn too hard – that was the job of the audiences – and the moment a busboy was allowed to ask for an autograph the place was destined for the dogs. Exclusive clubs were where stars went to get away from that sort of thing.

That moment had yet to come. For the time being the Crystal Heart was the place to be.

The band had a great deal to do with it. They beat good rhythm and the horn section had a sensuality to it that would have had Martin Quigley shedding his trousers and making a beeline for the dance floor.

That was where Fabio saw Elizabeth, spinning at the centre of a crowd of adoring onlookers.

At first he was quite convinced that it wasn't Elizabeth at all – couldn't be, in fact – but he spotted Frankie Nayland brooding at a table in the corner and, as much as his eyes doubted what they were seeing, he had known the woman long enough. This was the Elizabeth he had first met, the firebrand, the sex siren. He had had no doubt that he could make a star of her – she was halfway there already. She had that rare ability that could never be taught: she made people stare. You just couldn't take your damned eyes off her. She was having the same effect on him now. He watched her dance as if she was the only woman in the room.

'Elizabeth!' said Henry, his latest protégé and the reason he was here tonight, getting the boy's face out and about as well as the promise of a 'chance meeting' for him (it had taken Fabio seven phone calls to arrange it) with Barbara Stanwyck.

'Sit down, you great ape,' said Fabio, yanking at the young man's coat-tails.

'But I want to dance!'

'The night is still young.'

Fabio stared at Elizabeth, catching every nuance of her performance. And it *was* a performance: she was working the crowd in the room just as surely as she did a camera lens. One thing he could never have criticised her for was her ability to sell herself. The fact that she was also as poisonous as a hatbox full of rattlesnakes was the unfortunate price you had to pay.

'How has she done it?'

'What?' asked Henry, unaware of anything but the beauty he saw before him.

'Never you mind.' Fabio caught Elizabeth's eye and waved. He gestured towards their table.

She smiled, then gave a slight nod.

Fabio looked over to Nayland, lost in the circle of revelry that surrounded him yet which never came close enough to touch him.

'Who's that?' asked Henry, following Fabio's gaze. 'He looks like he's at a funeral.'

'Perhaps he is,' Fabio replied. 'That's the husband of the woman you slept with. Maybe you should go and introduce yourself.'

Henry laughed. 'No, thanks. Anyway, I thought their marriage was a sham.'

'In this town what isn't?' Elizabeth was making her way towards them. 'Now do me a favour, Henry, my boy, and make yourself scarce for five minutes.'

'I want to talk to her.'

'And I'm sure you will, but not now. First business and then pleasure. She and I have things to discuss. Scram.'

Henry sighed but did as he was told, though not before stepping in close to Elizabeth and whispering in her ear. Whatever he said must have amused her greatly because she laughed loudly enough to challenge the clarinet player as he tried to channel Benny Goodman.

'He likes you,' said Fabio as she sat down.

'Who doesn't?' Elizabeth replied, taking a glass from the table next to them and pouring herself some of Fabio's champagne.

'So, this is the result of your new regime?'

'Indeed it is. Are you impressed?'

'Spellbound. And cynical . . . Frankie wouldn't tell me how you'd managed it.'

'Dear Frank, such a gentleman to keep a lady's secrets.'

'I don't like secrets.'

'And yet your career is built on them.'

Fabio conceded that point by raising his glass. 'All right, let me rephrase it: I don't like secrets kept from *me*.'

'Does it matter? Do I look good?'

'You look wonderful.'

'Good enough for you to get me work?'

'There's still the problem with your accent . . .'

'To hell with my accent. With looks like there do you really think an audience cares?'

'As self-effacing as ever.'

'And honest.'

'Yes.' Fabio took a sip of his drink, pretending that he needed to think. Elizabeth didn't believe it for a moment but was gracious enough to allow him the showmanship. 'Fine,' he said. 'You look great. The camera will love you as it always did.'

'So you'll get to work?'

'Naturally.'

'I don't want rubbish, Fabio. I want big pictures. This is a comeback and it has to be huge.'

He laughed. 'You never did want much. Anything else?'

'Yes.' She looked over towards Henry who was making his way towards the bar. 'I want him.'

'Greedy.'

'You think I make a good match with Frank any more? Let's be honest, he'll be a weight around my neck. I need you to find a way to sell our divorce.'

'The Great American Public doesn't like divorce.'

'It's your job to make them like it. I want Henry.'

'Do his feelings come into it?'

'Don't be an idiot. Since when did you worry about things like that? You want your boy to make it big and I'm offering you the chance to get that. You win twice over.'

That was certainly true. Fabio looked over towards Henry who had now been joined by Nayland. He could guess what they were likely to be talking about.

'When Nayland gets nasty,' he said, '– and he will, you know he will – does he have anything on you that could be a problem?'

'Like what?' Elizabeth smiled, a passable imitation of innocence.

'Don't play games with me, Elizabeth. You wanted to talk business, so fine, we're talking business. Can Nayland damage you?'

'He never would.'

'Don't assume. He loves you, you know that. You think he's just going to roll over and let you do what you want?'

Elizabeth drained her champagne and stood up. 'Of course. That's what Frank's for.'

She turned to leave and then remembered

something. 'Don't forget the party, will you?'

'How could I forget?'

'Make sure we both have something to celebrate.'

She swayed her way back to the dance floor and Fabio felt a sharp pain in his belly. Goddamn the woman, she always made him nervous. She was lethal, always had been. He could talk to Nayland, maybe get him to see the business sense in a divorce. After all, if it was played right it would bring them both some much-needed publicity. Still, Fabio knew him better than that. Nayland didn't care about much but he certainly cared about Elizabeth. If that was taken away from him then who knew what he would do?

Fabio's guts ached. Things were about to get deeply unpleasant. For the first time in his fifty-odd years he felt a passing pang for the simple world of his youth.

'I saw you talking to my wife.'

Henry, his mind on nothing more complex than a spritzer, turned around to find himself face to face with Frank Nayland.

'As long as that's all you saw me do,' he replied, intending to joke his way out of the situation. Nayland clearly didn't see the funny side, scowling in open disgust.

'You admit it, then?' he said. His voice was slurred and Henry realised he was facing a man who was definitely on the wrong side of a bottle of whiskey.

He was a big man, the unfit side of forty, yes, but Henry wasn't stupid enough to think that would make him a pushover if things got out of hand.

'I was just making a joke,' he replied, trying to make his voice sound as calm and reassuring as he could. 'I didn't mean anything by it.'

'By what?' Nayland was not in the mood to be talked down to and people on either side of them were beginning to pay close attention, there was nothing a party crowd liked more than scandal and upset. 'She was just a one-night affair – is that what you're telling me?'

'Whoa there! I wasn't saying anything like that.'

'Oh, so you plan on making a habit of it, then? And I'm supposed to just stand by and allow it, am I?'

'Look, this is getting out of control.' Henry raised his hands. 'You said you saw me talking to your wife, I joked about it. I don't know what you're after from me but there's no fight here.'

'You expect me to believe that you only talked to her? What about last night? I saw the two of you together. Until you both vanished, that is.' Nayland started to step closer, wanting to loom over the shorter man. The drink made him unsteady, though, and he swayed a little, knocking into a group of people who were sipping at their cocktails and pretending not to listen.

'Hey,' said one of them, turning around to address Nayland directly. 'Steady on, old feller. You made me spill my drink.'

Nayland turned to look at the man, screwing up his eyes in an attempt to focus.

'I know you,' he announced. 'You're that queer who prances about with a sword.'

The man's expression lost all semblance of politeness, turning into a snarl. 'If you want to embarrass yourself in public, then feel free. But I'll ask you to leave the rest of us out of it.'

'Look,' said Henry, still foolishly convinced that the situation could be defused with a few soothing words. 'Let's just calm down. This is stupid – nobody wants a fight here.'

'Speak for yourself, you cuckolding little shit!' roared Nayland and punched him as hard as he could on the nose.

Henry went down fast, not having expected the blow. Unfortunately he managed to take a young woman and her partner with him as he fell.

'You drunk idiot!' said the man Nayland had insulted, channelling the screen hero he so often played and getting a punch of his own in. Nayland was more prepared than Henry had been and he managed to deflect the main force of it, flailing his arms and shoving his attacker backwards into the crowd. He hadn't finished with Henry yet, though, and, when the young man sat upright, dabbing at his bleeding nose, Nayland got a solid kick in, sending him back down, yelping with pain.

That was the last blow that Nayland managed to land. From that point on he was surrounded by people only too happy to take him down.

He struggled as someone pinned his arms against his side while somebody else sneaked a low punch to his gut which took the wind and impetus out of him. After that it was all he could do not to throw up the last few rounds he'd drunk onto his attackers.

'Frank!' Elizabeth shouted as she appeared.

Even though she'd called his name Nayland wasn't blind to the fact that it was Henry she ran to, helping him up and dabbing at his bleeding face with a napkin snatched from a waiter.

There was the blinding pulse of a couple of flashbulbs and Frank Nayland realised he had just made another in a long history of stupid mistakes.

Detective Scott Harrison (consistently referred to as 'Scotty' by his friends, despite his best attempts to discourage it) did not like movies. In this he found himself in a select club of one, surrounded by friends and colleagues who made great sport of goading him over the fact.

'Jesus but you're a miserable son of a bitch,' they would say. 'Lighten up and enjoy yourself once in a while.'

Harrison had no difficulty doing just that. He simply preferred to do so in a manner that didn't involve flickering pictures of ego-driven idiots acting out stories in which he had precious little interest. It wasn't a case of his being miserable, he just didn't understand the fuss. When cinema had first dragged its unwieldy self into being, he had watched as excessively made-up actors mimed their grotesque way across the screen and had wondered precisely what he was supposed to be impressed about.

'It's like they're in the room with you!' his wife had said. Infuriatingly, she was a great devotee of the medium.

'Except they can't speak, respond or tell a story using their mouths,' Harrison had replied. 'If I want to see a mime show I'll head down the park.'

Then the talkies had arrived and he was dragged along again to see this latest innovation. He sat bored while Bela Lugosi professed his admiration for the 'creatures of the night'.

'See?' his wife had said. 'Now they can talk! Do you get it now?'

'I see they've taken one of the all-time classics – a book about sensuality, violence and honour – and reduced it to a Hungarian in too much make-up moaning at a cocktail party,' he replied.

His wife had washed her hands of him after that and now went to the pictures with her friends, despairing of him ever seeing the positive side of the medium.

His recent move to the West Coast had therefore been something of a kick in the teeth for him as he was now utterly immersed in a world of which he understood little. It had done nothing to change his mind. In his opinion, anyone in the movies was a egomaniacal waste of space and if he could only have locked the lot of them up and returned home to the cool, familiar streets of New York he would have been a happy man indeed.

That seemed depressingly unlikely to happen but now, standing in the bar of the utterly horrible Crystal Heart, he wanted it more than ever.

'He just went wild,' a man was bleating in his ear, no doubt someone he was supposed to know. 'I just bet he was on drugs.'

Harrison looked the man in the eye. 'You think I should be searching everyone here for illicit sub-stances?' he asked. 'That what you're saying?' Pre-dictably enough, the little man's bravado crumpled instantly and he shoved his hands into his pockets.

'No, no, I'm sure that won't be necessary. I mean, it was only Frank Nayland who was out of control, wasn't it? Nobody else was misbehaving.'

'Then it was a rare night in Hollywood,' Harrison replied, moving away from the irritating fellow and over to his partner.

'All good fun, eh, Scotty?' his colleague said, his

smile, as always, big enough to take a bite out of the wall. Harrison's partner, a short fat man called Brunswick, was another reason why Harrison had grown to truly hate his job. The man was a walking gland of enthusiasm, for *anything*. He ate as though the government had just announced a ban on food, drank like alcohol was the antidote to a poison he had been injected with and walked around the streets in a constant state of glee as he recognised every face he encountered.

'It's a waste of time,' Harrison said. 'So some ageing ham took a swing at another – who cares?'

'Frank Nayland wasn't a ham,' Brunswick insisted. 'Did you never see him in *Walk of Fire*? The man was an idol.'

'With clay feet.'

Brunswick looked confused at that, not understanding the reference. 'No idea . . .' he replied, not wanting to admit his ignorance.

'It means he had an inherent weakness,' Harrison said. 'It's from the Bible.'

'Oh yeah, like *The Ten Commandments*. I loved that movie.'

'Of course you did.' Harrison was quick to change the subject. 'Anyway, there's nothing for us to do here. It's not like anybody's going to press charges.'

'I don't know – he fetched the kid one hell of a punch.'

'Right now somebody's agent is talking to somebody else's agent, they're both going to be having a breakfast meeting with someone from the studios and before you know it we'll hear about how they've all kissed and made up.'

'I can't see that happening. Nayland was pretty pissed at the guy.'

'If he'd been sleeping with my wife I would have been pissed too. Mind you, if he'd been sleeping with my wife he'd already have suffered worse than anything I could offer.'

Brunswick smiled dutifully at the joke.

'Anyway,' Harrison continued, 'the point is that these boys are commodities, just like motor cars, and you don't sell something unless you can convince the public that it's safe and what they want. In a couple of days you'll be hearing how it was a terrible mistake, I guarantee it.'

'What about the maid?'

'The maid?'

'You didn't hear about that? It was Grierson's case; Nayland's maid went missing a couple of days ago. They took her out, apparently, some night on the tiles to apologise for an accident at work . . .'

'That doesn't sound right.'

'Yeah, I didn't believe it either but the house - keeper corroborates the story and they were seen all over the place so Grierson's running with it. Anyway, Nayland drops her off but it's the wrong address – the girl's lied to him because she doesn't want him to see where she really lives. Then she never arrives home.'

'And Grierson believes all this?'

'He's got loads of eyewitnesses who back the story up, even one of the press boys who took a shot of them over at the Tip-Top Club. Though to be honest with you the picture's so damned blurred it could be of anybody.'

'How do you know all this?'

'Well, you know, it's Nayland and Elizabeth Sasdy, isn't it? You pay attention!'

'Do you? I couldn't care less.'

'Oh come on! You must like Elizabeth Sasdy! She's a real dame.'

'The wife? She's trouble, she's got it written all over her.'

'But in such beautiful handwriting.'

Harrison decided to drop it. It was no business of his and if he had to listen to any more of Brunswick's enthusiasm he'd end up with a headache. What did he care about a missing maid?

In time he would grow to care a great deal.

NEWSPAPERS APPEAR ON-SCREEN ONCE AGAIN:

'FRANK NAYLAND RELIVING HIS ACTION DAYS IN BAR BRAWL!'

'DOWN AND OUT! IS FRANK NAYLAND WASHED UP?'

'JEALOUSY HITS AGING STAR IN NIGHT-CLUB PUNCH-UP!'

All unflattering type is further nailed home with a selection of pictures of Nayland looking far from his best. Bloated and bemused, spread wide by those around him as they attempt to haul him away from his intended victim.

Nayland is once again a talked-about actor. However much he may wish otherwise.

'Well, that's just wonderful!' Fabio sighed, dumping the pile of newspapers in front of Nayland. 'Like we needed this.'

'I'm sorry.'

'You will be by the time I've finished dealing with you. Jesus, Frankie, what were you thinking?'

'I wasn't. Well . . .' Nayland rubbed at his face, trying to force the hangover out of his pores. 'You know, I was just jealous.'

'This is Elizabeth we're talking about, for Christ's sake, a woman who has more affairs than I have digestion pills. What's suddenly made the difference?'

'I don't know, I guess it just hit me . . . I'm sick of sharing her.'

'I hate to tell you this, Frankie, but she was never yours in the first place. You know how this kind of thing works: it was a marriage of convenience, a business arrangement. This was not white lace and red roses.'

'I know.' Nayland clenched his fist and rapped it on the table, a move he immediately regretted because his hand was so swollen that it felt like punching a knife. 'You think I don't know that? The whole thing is a lie.'

'Damn right it is. And now it's a lie that's got to stop.'

That knocked Nayland harder than anything else so far. He stared at Fabio in genuine confusion. 'What do you mean?'

'I mean we need to arrange a divorce. I can't work with the two of you like this.'

'A divorce? What are you talking about, a divorce?'

'Last night more than helped, Frankie. You're backing me into an impossible situation here. With Elizabeth's new looks I need to make a fresh start with her. I certainly don't need an abusive alcoholic husband to contend with – how am I supposed to make good press out of that?'

Nayland couldn't believe he was hearing this. 'I'm not abusive . . . I'm not a bloody alcoholic, either. Don't tell me you can't paper over the cracks on this, I know you can, just like you have whenever one of your other clients has got in a little trouble.'

'Yeah,' said Fabio, 'I can sort this out, I can also make Elizabeth's comeback bigger and better than ever, but I can't do both at the same time.' He shifted in his seat, sweating because of both the heat of the morning and the stress of dealing with his business.

'Listen carefully,' he said. 'Let me spell out to you how this works. I can launch Elizabeth back into the business but it will be a *launch* – nobody's seen her on a screen for close to five years. I'm starting afresh here. I can do that but right now when I'm trying to talk about her the papers are going to be talking about *you* – you see that, right? If you're a couple then you share the column inches. I need a clear voice, one beautiful note about a woman making her return to show business. I don't need every other paragraph bringing up the fact that her husband has a drink problem.'

'I don't have a drink problem!'

'Frankie, it doesn't matter what you have. If the papers have decided you're a drunk then, until they get bored, you're a drunk. You know how this game works – we're selling stories here and I have to control those stories. So here's how it's going to have to be:

'I release the story that the two of you are separated. That you're going to seek help for your addiction—'

Nayland began to speak again, incensed at this rubbish. If either of them had an addiction it wasn't him! Fabio held up his hand.

'Please, Frankie, we've worked together for years and my back's against the wall here. I want to keep helping you but I need you to listen and not talk right now, OK?'

Nayland, his head throbbing, nodded.

'So . . . you vanish for a little while, getting help. In the meantime I make a big fuss about Elizabeth, the beautiful young woman emerging from the ashes of her marriage and her period out of work – she's the fairy-tale princess, making good in a hard world. They'll love it. Then, in six months or so we bring you back into the limelight, a reformed character, a man who has battled his demons and won. Actually . . .' Fabio laughed, 'now I come to say that out loud I realise this was what we should always have done. Nothing better than a man returned from the edge, heroic, noble . . . We could have you playing the loners, the wise father figures, the men who've seen it all and lived to tell the tale. The studios will love you.'

'I don't care about the studios,' insisted Nayland. 'I care about my marriage. I'm not leaving Elizabeth.'

'Don't make this hard on all of us, Frankie,' said Fabio, 'besides, you don't have a choice. I built that into the paperwork years ago, remember? At the time it was you that insisted on it. You both had the right to walk out of the marriage if it proved detrimental to your career. Right now that clause couldn't be more appropriate. I need you as two separate clients again, not a unit.'

'Elizabeth won't agree to this.'

'Don't be an idiot, Frankie, of course she will. She knows common sense when she hears it.'

Fabio chose not to mention that it had been Elizabeth's idea in the first place, he failed to see how that would help matters. Much better if the whole thing was kept on the footing of a business deal. If he had any chance of keeping Nayland under control it would be by making the whole thing cold and contractual. On the spur of the moment he decided that a little false hope wouldn't go amiss, either.

'Besides, who says it has to be permanent? We break you up, start again, build you both up in the public eye and then the icing on the cake: Hollywood's greatest tortured couple settle their differences and fall in love all over again! Imagine that! The chicks will be crying their eyes out.'

'So stupid.'

'Maybe, but it works and you know it. You need to take a holiday, we retire you for a few months, then – BOOM – you're back and fighting fit. You got anywhere you could go?'

Nayland was slowly seeing all the ramifications here. 'This is my house!'

'It's the house you both live in, Frankie, just bricks and mortar. I figured it would be better if you were to head away for a while. Hey! You ever been to Europe?'

'Fabio, I'm English, I was born there.'

'Oh yeah . . . I always forget Britain's in Europe. Probably because they do, too.'

'I'm going nowhere. Besides, Elizabeth needs me.'

'She does, and what she needs more than anything is for you to agree to this.'

'I can't believe this . . .'

Fabio decided to fall back on the bullshit again. 'Come on, Frankie, it's what? Six months? A year at the outside. You break up, then I bring you back together. Fairy tale. Beautiful.'

Nayland was silent so Fabio decided to press the advantage. 'Great. I'll get the paperwork written up. You won't regret it, Frankie. You know what they say: sometimes you have to knock something down so as to build it back up stronger.'

At least, he thought people probably said that. If they didn't they should.

'You just wait, Frankie my boy, the best times are still ahead. I just need you to trust me and do as I tell you. Why have a dog and bark yourself, huh?'

When Nayland finally saw Elizabeth she appeared so happy that he was under no illusion about where she had spent the night. Normally this would have made him all the angrier but now, having stewed in self-pity and fatalism for a couple of hours, he was beyond it. He had also given up on his hangover, deciding that the only safe way to proceed was to drink some more.

Elizabeth had taken precautions this time, hiding her face by the judicious use of a wide-brimmed hat, a large pair of sunglasses and a scarf. A Cinderella returning from her ball, she had no intention of blowing her new reputation by revealing how old she really was. No, not even that, Nayland realised as she removed her disguise. If her reversion to a 'natural' state the last time she had used the blood had seemed to add a couple of years to her age, then this time it was more like five.

'Dear God,' he said, 'just look at what it's doing to you.'

She simply shrugged as she headed towards her master bathroom. 'Now I have the cure why should I care?' She stopped and gave him a piercing look. 'You're still drunk.'

'Not quite. I took a few hours to sober up in between.'

Nayland followed her into the bathroom,

ignoring her look of disgust and sitting down on the lid of the toilet to watch as she shed her blouse and stood in front of the mirror.

'Have you nothing to say?' she asked, raising the small bottle of blood and pouring some into the sink.

'You want an apology?'

'I think I'm owed one. After all we've been through you then cause a scene like that and threaten everything.'

He nodded. 'Yes, Fabio's already explained to me how it's all my fault. He says we have to get a divorce for the sake of our careers.'

Elizabeth had dabbed a flannel in the blood and had been about to apply it to her face. She paused. 'And what did you say?'

Nayland gave a humourless laugh. 'Not surprised, then? No "My God, Nayland, we can't do that!" or "Who does he think he is?" Just "And what did you say?"'

She didn't answer, just stared at him for another second before continuing to apply the blood as if it were nothing but liquid foundation.

'I said no, of course,' Nayland continued, 'but he made it clear that wasn't an option. He reminded me that our marriage was nothing but a business arrangement and that we needed to continue to think of it in such terms. He also insisted that our separation needn't be permanent.'

Elizabeth had coated half of her face in the blood now. When she stared at Nayland it was with the nightmarish face of a Japanese kabuki performer. 'Just tell me what he said.'

Nayland did so, admittedly placing a lot more emphasis on the temporary nature of the agreement than Fabio had done. 'He thinks it's the only way to stage-manage both our careers.'

'It sounds sensible enough to me.'

'It would, wouldn't it? You're not the one who has to admit to being a drunk and vanish off the face of the Earth for six months.'

'Don't exaggerate, Frank darling. You don't have to vanish completely, just carry on as you always did. Before all this nobody had seen hide nor hair of us for years – nothing's changed, really.'

Elizabeth's face was now completely painted and she continued to daub the blood down her neck and across her shoulders and chest.

'So you don't see a problem, then?'

She shrugged. 'Of course not. We do as Fabio says – he's never let us down in the past. As far as I can tell he's talking great sense: this time next year we'll be back at the top again.'

'We?'

She turned and looked at him, offering a clear smile from within the charnel house of the rest of her face. 'Frank, you know that I'll never be faithful to you, I'm simply incapable of it – you've always known that. This marriage is, as Fabio says, a business arrangement.'

'A beautiful public face hiding something grotesque beneath? That's rather becoming the theme of our existence, isn't it?'

Elizabeth turned back to the mirror. 'I shan't dignify that with a reply and if you're going to be horrid you can just get out now.' She painted down to her midriff, coating her breasts liberally before extending her work out to her arms and hands.

'And will that be part of the agreement, I wonder?' Nayland asked. 'Will I have to leave here?'

'I don't see why, though you might want to rent somewhere for the sake of appearances. It hardly looks right if we divorce and then you're still bumbling around the place.'

She stood for a moment, arms wide, letting the blood dry.

'I certainly won't kick you out,' she added, 'so don't worry about that.'

'Really?' He was pathetically relieved to hear that.

'Of course not. You know how much I need you.' She smiled again. 'We're a partnership, Frank, and we always will be. What does a piece of paper matter?'

He nodded. 'I'll sign the papers.'

'So will I. Now help me off with the rest of my clothes, would you? Then I'll get in the bath and you can shower me off.'

Nayland got up and did as she'd asked, albeit with rather fumbling fingers, the drink having robbed him of his usual dexterity. She made no complaint, happy to have him in his correct position: the agreeable servant.

Elizabeth climbed into the bathtub and knelt down. 'Now spray me, darling. Let's see if it's done its job.'

He took the extendable hose and slowly sluiced the blood away, rubbing softly at her skin like a mother bathing a child.

In a few minutes she was clean and the blood had worked its magic. It was perhaps even more baffling when seen on only half the canvas. Her upper body looked so different from what lay below her waist, though Nayland realised he didn't love either half more than the other – he was far too hopelessly devoted for that. He adored every corrupt inch of her.

'It worked,' he said. 'Worked perfectly.'

Elizabeth got up and moved to the mirror, smiling to see herself restored once more. 'There I am,' she said.

'Yes,' he agreed. 'There you are.'

'Wonderful. That means you won't have to go every single day. Every other day should be fine.'

'Wonderful,' Nayland echoed, his voice as dead as the women who were to come.

'Don't worry, Frank,' she said, cupping his head

with her wet, perfect hand. 'Everything will carry on just as it should.'

[MONTAGE]

The soundtrack swells and the screen goes dreamy as we cross-fade from Elizabeth's bathroom to Nayland behind the wheel of his car. He is once more wearing his disguise.

We see a succession of prostitutes getting into his car, one cross-fading into another and into another again . . .

Nayland smiles but his heart is not in it. The camera lingers on the cold, dead look in his eyes.

Still he drives, still he does as he's told.

We see the barn, so innocent-looking from the outside, sheltered by its orchard of orange trees.

BANG! We jump-cut to Elizabeth, her face looking older than ever as she moves in towards the camera, a straight razor in her hand. We see the blade in close-up: it glints in the light. SWISH! It cuts down towards the screen in a shower of blood.

Elizabeth laughs and her old face fades into an image of her drenched in blood, which then fades again as we see her laughing, beautiful once more.

The camera pulls back and we see that she is at yet another party, surrounded by those who adore her. She is looking off-screen and the camera follows her, focusing on the handsome face of Henry, standing back a little to give her space.

Another cut, this time to the wall of Henry's hotel room. His face and Elizabeth's come into shot from either side of the frame, kiss, then topple backwards as they fall onto the bed in a lovers' clinch.

We cross-fade to the car once more, Nayland taking a swig from a hip flask as he cruises the sleazier areas of Los Angeles.

P.O.V. We are looking through an innocent victim's eyes as she moves towards the car and leans in through the window. Nayland smiles at us: it is the watery smile of a drunk.

BANG! The razor again: another victim of Elizabeth's beauty.

A newspaper spins into frame, its headline screaming at us as it fills the screen:

HOLLYWOOD DIVORCE! BEAUTY AND THE BEAST SEPARATED!

Another:

'I AM SO GLAD TO BE FREE!' SAYS ELIZABETH SASDY, BOX-OFFICE QUEEN

Another:

'I NEED TIME TO SORT MYSELF OUT.' FRANK NAYLAND ADMITS HIS ADDICTION

Finally we see Fabio, looking on as Elizabeth once more dances the night away at one of the hottest spots in town. The camera closes in on him, ending with an extreme close-up. This is a man who is ill at ease. He knows that all is not well . . .

FADE TO BLACK

'So,' said Henry, his mouth full of scrambled eggs, 'you going to this party tonight?'

'Of course I'm going,' Fabio replied, staring suspiciously into the depths of his muddy coffee. 'My groin hasn't been this excited for years.'

'An image that I could have done without, thanks.'

'Then avert your eyes this evening, kid. Elizabeth's parties are not for the faint-hearted, the prudish or those lacking in stamina.'

'Sounds wonderful and terrifying, all at the same time.'

'Just as all great things in life should.'

'How are things going with them? You know, the divorce and stuff.'

'Not that you have a vested interest.'

Henry smiled. 'Just asking.'

'Yeah, and don't think I haven't noticed how much time you've been spending with her.'

A worrying, dreamy look came into Henry's eyes. 'She's one hell of a woman.'

'An appropriate description for sure. Just you watch yourself.'

'I thought you were all for it?'

Fabio sighed and took a sip of his coffee. As a

businessman he certainly was all for it – in fact, it was perfect. What better way of shooting his new protégé to stardom than by putting him on Elizabeth's arm? After all, it had worked before. Still, he would be lying if he didn't admit to feeling a bit guilty about it: Henry was a good kid and didn't have the first idea what he was getting into. Or maybe he was patronising him, maybe he could hold his own. He had the years on Elizabeth, that was for sure. His shelf life would be longer, however good she was looking. Nature had to take its course sooner or later, didn't it?

'I am,' he said eventually. 'My two brightest stars shining together – what could be better?'

'So how long do you think it will take?'

'I don't know. We're pushing Nayland's behaviour as justifiable cause and there's more than one judge that owes me a favour. What's the rush?'

'I thought you wanted to cash in, you know, you're the one that's always saying you should strike while the iron's hot.'

'You listen to everything I say, huh?'

'Of course. Doesn't mean I pay it any mind.' Henry laughed and Fabio took the opportunity to change the subject, returning to pipe dreams of ideal roles for Henry. If there was one thing Fabio had learned in his years as a manager it was that there was no subject actors liked discussing more than themselves.

They finished breakfast and he sent Henry on his way, choosing to ignore the spring in the young man's step. He was a dramatic contrast to the car crash that was Frank Nayland. It was the law of nature, Fabio told himself, survival of the fittest: one alpha male fell by the wayside to be replaced by the next.

Except nature didn't seem to be playing entirely fair with the queen of the pack, did it?

And that was something he simply had to get his head around before things developed any further.

Whatever he had said to Elizabeth he had no intention of letting her keep her secret. On the one hand, if there was a way for ageing actresses to tap into the fountain of youth he wanted to know how it worked because the knowledge would be worth a fortune. On the other, and this was by far his greatest compulsion, secrets were certainly his business, as Elizabeth herself had said – but only when he knew the details of them. You got nowhere through ignorance in this life – half his business dealings hinged on that fact. Knowledge was a currency and he needed to have as much of it as he could.

Already Fabio had been paying close attention to Elizabeth's movements, not just at night when she was now a mainstay of the party scene but also when she thought nobody was looking. That was where he would find out what he really needed to know: when she thought she was safe.

He had met up with Patience. In fact, that had been his first step.

'How does she do it?' he had asked her bluntly, seeing no mileage in small talk.

'I couldn't say, I'm sure.'

'Can't or won't? Because let's have no confusion over loyalty here: she may be your mistress but I'm the one that got you the job. You work for me as well as her.'

Patience hadn't responded favourably to that, no doubt because she knew it to be true. Fabio had recruited the entire household staff that supported Elizabeth and Nayland. He had selected them from the agencies, he still paid their wages, they were an expense that went through his books. He owned them as surely as he did the two stars whom they served.

'I just don't know,' Patience had insisted. 'I barely see her these days. She's always either in her room, partying or driving around.'

'Driving?' Elizabeth was not, as far as Fabio could recall, a woman who had ever taken much pleasure in getting anywhere under her own steam. She was a woman who liked to be driven.

'She goes out most days, I couldn't say where. Heads out after lunch, then comes back a few hours later.'

'You think she's going to a clinic or something?'

Patience had shrugged. 'Maybe. To be honest, I

assumed she was seeing her young man.'

'Her young man?'

'I read the papers same as everyone else, I know what she gets up to.'

Except you don't, Fabio had thought, *or I wouldn't have to be digging this out of you piece by damned piece.* 'Why did you think that?'

'She dresses up, you know, hiding herself with big sunglasses and the like. She looks like she doesn't want to be recognised – isn't that how people behave when they're going to see their secret lovers?'

'Except he's hardly secret, is he?' And Elizabeth was not the sort of woman to hide her face either, Fabio thought. She was not a woman who covered herself, however illicit her business. So what was she hiding?

'I don't know about any of it,' Patience had said with finality. 'I just do my job and that's all I think about.'

'Which is why you're such good value,' Fabio admitted. 'Forget I asked.'

And she probably would. She was the most discreet woman he had ever met in this country, the perfect servant. But Fabio wouldn't let the matter drop as easily as she seemed able to. He would chase this thing down to the end.

Which was why he decided to hire a car and follow Elizabeth himself. It was better that way because then only he would know whatever it was that he found out. Knowledge was a currency indeed, he reminded himself, and the fewer the people who possessed it the more valuable it was.

Fabio drove over to Elizabeth's house, resigned to a possible wait. The odds of catching her in the act were good, though, he decided. Patience had said that Elizabeth tended to go out after lunch and if what she was up to had something to do with her appearance (and for the life of him he couldn't think of an alternative explanation) then she would certainly be about her business today. If there was a time when she would want to look at her very best it would be at the party.

He parked off the road, a short way up from Elizabeth and Nayland's main drive, and settled down with a handful of scripts that he had been sent by various studios. Most of them were unworkably shoddy, he decided as he flicked through their pages. More monster madness from Universal, some wild nonsense about werewolves in London (who gave two shits about London? Werewolves in Los Angeles, yes, he could have got behind that as an idea) and a melodrama about a homeless woman who got embroiled with a criminal gang, the sort of thing that would once have had Mary Pickford written all over it. He could certainly do better and there was no harm in holding out for juicier roles for his clients. The studios respected a man who said no – up to a point, at least.

Fabio was threatening to doze off, the midday heat hitting the roof of the car and sending him into a sweaty stupor, when he heard a car approaching. He shrunk down in his seat, looking for all the world like a low-rent private detective in a B-movie. It wasn't Elizabeth, it was Nayland, though he seemed to be going to some considerable effort to disguise the fact. It was all Fabio could do not to laugh – the guy was wearing a false beard! And he thought *he*'d been ridiculous burrowing into the collar of his coat to avoid detection. At least he'd left the kiddies' dress-up kit at home. What the hell could Nayland be doing in that get-up?

Fabio made a split decision, turned on the ignition and pulled his car out onto the road. He hadn't intended to take any interest in Nayland's movements but this was too good to ignore. He was up to something for sure and Fabio couldn't have lived with himself if he'd passed up the oppor - tunity to find out what. According to Patience, Elizabeth went out most days so it wasn't as if he wouldn't get his chance to follow her again.

He kept his distance, though the way Nayland had been the last couple of weeks he was pretty sure he could have ridden the guy's bumper and he wouldn't have noticed. The man was not at his peak right now.

They cut down through the hills and towards the city. Fabio hoped Nayland wasn't planning on driving for hours – he'd be furious if this whole thing turned out to be a wild-goose chase. Still, that beard drew him on: what could Nayland be doing that needed a disguise? It occurred to him that Patience's assumption that Elizabeth was meeting up with a lover could turn out to be accurate about her husband. Was Nayland meeting someone on the side? Hell, not even on the side any more . . . Surely not. It wasn't as though he had to worry about being caught: if he was bedding some gal he'd have been full of it the last time they'd talked. Why would he hide it? Unless it wasn't a gal . . .? Oh Christ, Fabio knew these English guys, they were all a bit weird when it came to sex. Might Nayland be seeing another *man*? If so he would hardly be the first Hollywood star to stray in that direction but it would be one hell of a bigger mess to cover up if that was what he was up to. Audiences didn't like their leading men to be nancies. Fabio could have believed it of Nayland but for one thing: his devotion to Elizabeth – the wet schmuck adored the poisonous bitch. He couldn't imagine him screwing anyone else, man or woman, given the way he felt for her.

So what was it?

As they entered the city it became a bit harder for

Fabio to follow Nayland as the traffic built around them and forced him to stick closer than he would have liked. Nayland gave no sign of having spotted him – in fact, he seemed to have enough problems just keeping on the road. The car had jerked violently a couple of times, once nearly hitting an old dame as she stepped off the sidewalk to cross the road.

'Watch where you're going, you blind bastard!' she shrieked, making Fabio laugh to hear such salty talk from a creature who looked like anyone's grandmother. Nayland gave no sign of having heard her. He just drove the car around a corner and continued cruising his way towards down - town. He was drunk, Fabio decided, that was why he was driving like such an idiot. So much for not having a problem with the bottle! Drunk in charge of a false beard – this was getting more interesting by the minute.

Soon they were in one of the sleazier districts and the traffic thinned out once more. Fabio hung back as Nayland began a slow crawl around the side streets.

'Jesus Christ,' he muttered, lowering the window slightly to let out some of the heat, 'don't tell me he came all this way shopping for hookers.'

It certainly looked that way as Nayland pulled up and beckoned a pair of girls over. Not the kind of ladies Fabio would have ever considered inserting a piece of himself into. They looked as rough as sailors and as classy as a dildo at a dinner party. Still, whatever turned you on . . . if Nayland liked them rough then Fabio could live with it, though he'd be insisting this client had regular medical checks if he was going to make a habit of indulging such tastes.

Fabio pulled in for a moment, watching as Nayland completed his transaction.

'Hey, honey?' called a voice from Fabio's passenger-side window. 'You looking for something?'

'Yeah,' he answered, lost in his own thoughts. He turned to look and his heart, that most ill-used and cold organ, almost thawed. The kid was no more than thirteen or so. 'Oh Christ,' he said, 'what are you doing out here? Go home to your mother, for God's sake.'

He lived in a world of sin but he had never become hardened to this. Didn't everyone deserve at least a few years of innocence before the world stripped them away? The one time he had ditched a client for moral reasons had been when he had found out that she liked boys on the wrong side of puberty. Let people wallow in whatever filth they choose but he'd have no part in that.

'Can't go home without a couple of dollars,' the kid said, 'or she'll beat me so hard I'll be out of work for a week.'

'Oh God . . .' Fabio grimaced at the thought and reached for his wallet. He pulled out five dollars. 'Take this and go home.' On reflection he snatched the note back for a moment. 'Even better,' he said, 'go somewhere else. Any mother lets you out here at your age is a no-good bitch and you should keep away from her.'

The girl shrugged. 'You gotta stick with your family,' she said, as if she was discussing a disagreement over seating arrangements at a wedding. 'They're all you got.'

He sighed and handed her the note. 'You don't need anyone but yourself, remember that. Just get out of here and take the night off, understand?'

She nodded, took the note and wandered off. No doubt she'd be back selling herself within the hour but there was nothing he could do about it.

He looked back over to Nayland in time to see his car turning the corner at the end of the street.

'Shit!' Fabio accelerated after him. He was damned if he was going to have driven all this way only to lose him now.

He nearly did. Turning along the next street he could see no sign of Nayland's car and it was a full three or four minutes before he spotted it at an intersection to his left, waiting for the lights to change. He resumed his careful tracking, creeping as close as the traffic allowed until they were on their way out of the city and he could relax a little, hanging back and keeping Nayland in sight a little way ahead.

So Nayland had come all the way over here just to pick up a couple of hookers? It just didn't make sense. He had enough contacts closer to home. Fabio was really starting to get a bad feeling about this. Something smelled bad and, determined as he was to find out what, he was beginning to suspect that the answer would create as many problems as it solved.

As they got closer to home, Nayland went past the turning that would have taken him back to his house and carried on up into the hills.

'Where the hell are you going now?' Fabio muttered.

Nayland pulled off the main road and onto a narrow dirt track. This presented Fabio with a problem: did he dare try and follow? Surely it would be obvious that he was tailing the man if he did so. He could hardly have a good reason for also using the track.

Deciding that caution was the only way forward – after all, he'd been careful up till now so why blow it at the last hurdle? – he drove a short way past and then pulled over.

He got out of the car and headed back to the start of the track. He began to walk along it.

It was hot as hell and he hoped to God that the trail wasn't miles long. He wasn't fit enough to be slogging along in this heat.

On both sides of the track was a dense orchard of orange trees and he decided to make life easier for himself by cutting through it. Besides, if Nayland reappeared he'd soon be caught if he was standing in the middle of the trail. He could hear the car ahead and it wasn't difficult to follow its engine sound.

The undergrowth was thick but he pushed his way through, cursing at the effect it was having on the legs of his suit's trousers and his patent leather shoes.

'Frankie, this had better be good,' he murmured as he trudged on.

He heard the car pull to a halt a short distance ahead. The doors opened and the previously quiet orchard was immediately ringing with the sound of raised female voices.

'I don't care how much you're paying,' said one. 'This ain't no summer house and I think you've been selling us a crock!'

You and me both, darling, Fabio thought as he got close enough to be able to see them through the trees. The track ended in front of a ramshackle-looking barn, not a destination Fabio would have ever imagined. Clearly the hooker agreed.

'I mean, this place is a dump! Who parties at a place like this?'

Fabio noticed another car parked next to

Nayland's, a smaller red coupe which he knew Elizabeth had favoured when she had decided – pointlessly, Fabio had thought – that she wanted a car of her own. So it looked like Nayland wasn't acting by himself: this was where she came as well. He could have saved himself a journey and come straight here if he had just been patient and waited for her to appear.

Nayland was giving a particularly ineffectual performance through the trees ahead. 'I told you it was out of the way,' he was saying in a rough New York accent. 'What's the problem?'

'The problem, mister, is my friend and I don't like working way out in the middle of nowhere when we don't even know who we're working with.'

'Then you shouldn't have got in the damned car, should you?' Nayland said, all trace of his accent now gone.

Fabio kept creeping closer, trying to make sure that he kept the trees between him and the group ahead.

'Joanie,' said the other girl, in a dazed, doped tone, 'I think we should go home now.'

Too late for that, thought Fabio. Nayland obviously agreed as he grabbed the first girl, the one that had a lot more edge to her voice, and began dragging her towards the barn.

'Let go of me!' she shouted. 'You don't get to just

muscle me around, mister!'

'I can do what I want,' said Nayland and, with one drunken lurch, he slammed the girl's head against the wall of the barn.

Oh fuck! thought Fabio. *What the hell have I stumbled on here?*

'Joanie?' called the doped girl. 'You all right, Joanie?'

The door of the barn opened and whatever concerns Fabio had had before were as nothing compared with the icy spread of terror he felt when he saw Elizabeth – at least, he assumed it was Elizabeth – appear in the doorway.

She was naked, which made the vision all the more horrible. Her skin hung in great folds, liver-spotted and ancient, and she looked like a woman near death as she lurched out of the door and made a grab for the dazed Joanie.

'Get the other one,' she told Nayland who silently did as he was told, walking towards the girl who was still standing by the car.

'Run, Betty, honey!' Joanie cried, her voice cracking, stifled by Elizabeth's yellowing fingers as they reached inside her mouth and grabbed at her tongue, trying to silence her.

Doped as she was, the urgency of Joanie's shout still woke Betty up and she did indeed make a break for it, running through the trees towards Fabio.

Oh Christ! He looked around, trying to decide what to do. Should he too make a run for it? If he did then he would certainly be seen.

He stayed put, more through indecision than anything else, fighting the urge to cry out as the girl tripped up and fell to the ground only a couple of feet away from him. He stayed hidden behind a tree, cursing himself for his cowardice but unwilling to step in to help even as Nayland grabbed the fallen girl by the hair and dragged her, screaming, back towards the barn.

'Oh God, oh God, oh God . . .' Fabio whispered, risking a glance around the tree and watching as Elizabeth and Nayland dragged the girls inside the barn. What the hell were they going to do? If it was the violent stuff they were after there were ways you could get it without resorting to all this.

And what was with Elizabeth? What he'd seen was not the beautiful sex siren he had spent the last couple of weeks promoting. With her looking like that he might have been able to partner her up with Karloff but that would be about her lot. How could she look so different?

He needed to know. He couldn't find out this much and then let go, it just wasn't in his nature.

Fabio moved through the trees, cutting around to the rear of the barn. There was a small window on the far side and if he could just get a quick glimpse through that . . .

He ran over to the wall, terrified now that he was exposed out in the open, and inched along towards the window. Inside, everyone sounded active: both girls were screaming, Elizabeth was shouting.

He reached the window and slowly, convinced he was going to find himself face to face with someone on the other side of the glass, he put one eye to it.

It was dark inside, a couple of lamps providing the only lighting. They were enough for Fabio to see Elizabeth and Nayland stringing one of the girls up from the ceiling by a length of chain.

'I said before,' Nayland was shouting, 'this is your half of the deal.'

'Grow a backbone,' Elizabeth replied – a sentiment Fabio could only agree with when applied to Nayland – 'I can't manage on my own.'

She made a good fist of it, though, as far as Fabio could tell. She tore the clothes from the dangling woman who had given up struggling now, her face puffy from the beating she had received.

'Just hold her steady,' Elizabeth demanded, turning her attentions to the other girl – Betty, Fabio reminded himself, the poor girl's name was Betty. Nayland did as he was told and Fabio bit his lip as Elizabeth picked up a stout length of wood and casually, almost carelessly, hit the woman over the head with it.

'There,' said Elizabeth, with no more emotion than if she'd just stamped on a beetle. 'I can manage from here. Get out if you can't bear to see what comes next.'

Fabio might well have taken that advice. But he couldn't tear his gaze away as the unnaturally aged woman dragged a metal bath beneath where Joanie had been strung up. Elizabeth climbed in the bath, her face right against the dangling woman's chest. She reached up and Fabio caught the glint of something metal and then Joanie was thrashing around violently. Elizabeth grabbed the woman's legs and yanked down. Blood was gushing from Joanie's throat now, drenching Elizabeth as she stood beneath. This was clearly part of the plan as, once the girl ceased her jerking around, Elizabeth let go of her and turned round under the crimson spray, massaging the blood all over her body like a woman taking a shower. She ran it through her hair before putting first one, then the other foot up on the edge of the bath so that she could rub the liquid along her legs. She tilted her head back and actually laughed as it ran, hot and thick, over her face.

Fabio understood. He didn't know how it was possible, had no logic to explain it, but it was clear that what he was seeing here was Elizabeth's 'new regime'. This was her secret. This was the source of her renewed beauty.

He had the proof of it after a few minutes when Elizabeth stepped out of the tub and over to a large watering can. She lifted it and tilted the spout over herself, washing the blood away to reveal fresh young skin.

Fabio didn't wait for the full revelation. He had seen enough. He was in terrible danger, he realised: anyone willing to do what he'd just witnessed wouldn't give his continued existence a second thought.

He headed back into the trees, moving around to the front of the barn as slowly and quietly as he could.

He could see Nayland, perched on the bonnet of a car, smoking a cigarette, looking like a man waiting contentedly for someone he was picking up from a train station. *You were even more broken than I realised*, thought Fabio. *Elizabeth? I could believe her capable of anything but I thought you were a better man than this.*

He kept moving away from the barn and once he felt he had put enough distance between them he broke into a run, his nerve finally snapping. He was half-convinced that Elizabeth would leap out at him at any moment, a blood-drenched demon from Hell, eager to pull him back down there.

When he got to the car he climbed in and drove away, constantly checking the rear-view mirror for any sign of pursuit.

He realised he was driving too fast as the car skidded a little on the tight corners and he forced himself to slow down. The last thing he needed to do was wreck the thing and find himself stuck out here.

The last thing he needed to do.

But what *was* he to do?

First things first. He headed home, dumping the car on his drive.

'Good afternoon, sir,' said Williams, his man-servant, as Fabio entered the house. 'Which suit would you like me to prepare for this evening?'

This evening.

The party.

Fabio ignored the man and ran straight to his drinks cabinet to see if it might hold some of the answers.

INTERTITLE: 'FABIO IS NOT THE ONLY ONE THINKING ABOUT ELIZABETH AND NAYLAND'

Detective Harrison was beginning to have very nasty thoughts indeed. They were complicated still further by the fact that nobody else in his department seemed to share them.

'Let it go, Scotty,' said Grierson, the detective who was supposed to be handling the case of Georgina Woolrich, the missing maid. 'There's nothing to it. She died of stupidity, walking around at that time of night. We'll find her body soon enough and that'll be that.'

'It's amazing that we have any criminals left,'

Harrison said, 'what with all the hard work this department does.'

'Screw you. You think you have time to do a better job, then by all means help yourself.' Grierson dumped a shamefully thin card folder on Harrison's desk and wandered outside to look menacingly at people for half an hour.

Harrison had gone through the few details of the Woolrich case. The blurry photograph, confiscated from one of the newspaper reporters, that alleged to show Georgina sitting with Frank Nayland and his wife was as useless as Brunswick had promised. It looked as if someone had jogged the photographer's arm. The faces were so indistinct as to be little but smears.

What was it about these people? Harrison wondered. Was it that their fame made them known quantities, above suspicion simply because 'That's Frank Nayland, we all know Frank, he wouldn't do something bad!'

Harrison had no such belief. As far as he could tell, the likes of Elizabeth Sasdy and Frank Nayland were only too capable of acting outside the law. Who could be surprised when even the police department seemed to encourage them to do so?

He had dug out Georgina's home address and decided to pay her family a visit.

He could see why the girl might have chosen to hide her real address, a run-down block that looked like it was one hard winter away from ruin. Looking along the row of houses, Harrison was reminded – as he so often was – of Hollywood fabrication. It looked like a film set, left out in the rain after filming had finished, abandoned to rot and crumble. This was the way of America, he decided, where the glamorous and the grotesque stood a few short miles from one another.

He headed up the steps to the front door and pressed the upstairs-apartment bell. There was no reply so he tried the door and wasn't in the least surprised when it swung open. Checking the lock he saw that the thing had been sheared in two.

Stepping inside, he found himself in a poky hallway, stairs leading up.

Already hot and sweaty from an afternoon of oppressive Los Angeles heat, he loosened his tie and began to climb.

The Woolriches' apartment was on the top floor, because God hated policemen just like everyone else did. Harrison was surprised by the immaculate door: gloss black paint with a carved crucifix fixed top centre. He was entering hallowed ground.

He rapped on the wood, trying not to smile at the jaunty jig this encouraged the wooden Jesus to perform as he rattled on his sacrificial nail.

The door was opened by a small woman who looked as if she suffered as much as the figure she had on her door. She was one of those women,

Harrison thought, who were so crushed by every-thing and everyone around them that they became smaller and smaller, juiceless raisins looking wist-fully back on the time when they had been grapes.

'Can I help you?' she asked in a somewhat querulous tone that suggested she would be terribly surprised if she could.

He showed her his ID. 'Detective Scott Harrison, LAPD. Just wanted to ask some follow-up questions about your daughter.'

She shrunk another inch. 'My poor Georgina. Do come in.'

The apartment inside rebuked him for his previous snobbery. It was immaculate and well cared for, a perfect illustration of a place where people had made the very best of what they had.

'Can I get you a drink of something?' she asked, 'I've made some iced tea if you like that.'

'I most certainly do and would love a glass. Thank you, Mrs Woolrich.'

She nodded, as much at his formality as his admission of thirst.

'Take a seat and I'll fix you a glass.'

Harrison did as he was told, choosing a straight-backed chair near the window. He looked around the room, noting the religious pictures on the walls – cheap iconography, some of them clipped from magazines, he suspected – and the sparse furniture. There was little sign of personality beyond the obvious love of the Lord. It was an apartment in which the family existed rather than lived.

'My husband isn't here, I'm afraid,' Mrs Woolrich said as she returned with his drink, placed alone on a large wooden tray. 'He doesn't really approve of my having visitors while he's out but I don't suppose he'll mind since you're the police.' Harrison took the drink. 'Though I will say he didn't take kindly to the previous detective – a Mr Grierson, I think he said his name was.'

Harrison took a mouthful of the drink and immediately relished it. He decided to be as open with the woman as possible, if only because she made good iced tea. 'Frankly, Mrs Woolrich, I don't take all that kindly to him, either. That's partly why I'm here.'

'He couldn't have been more dismissive of our Georgina had he tried,' she said, taking a seat opposite Harrison. 'I think he had already decided what she was like and no amount of facts to the contrary would sway him from that opinion.'

It was a fair judgement and he told her so. 'That's why I decided to take a little look into things. I don't want to give any false hope, it's perfectly possible that my colleague is right. Still, I felt it warranted a little more attention than it was given.'

Mrs Woolrich nodded and looked out on the street. 'He was convinced she would be ashamed of living here. Maybe she is.' She paused, reflected, then corrected her tense. 'Was. I really don't think there's much point in hoping she's still with us, do you?'

Harrison continued with his policy of honesty. 'No, I'm afraid not. I think we would have found her before now if that was the case.'

She nodded. 'Are you a religious man, Detective?'

'Not really, my mother was but . . . I don't know, this job sometimes makes you forget the higher concerns.'

'I can imagine. Still, you should look to your God – he can be a great help at times. I'm sure he's looking after Georgina now.'

'That must be a relief.'

'For her as well as for us. Still, it's earthly matters that concern you. We must hope that whoever hurt her can be found so that they may not do so to another poor girl.'

'That would be my hope.'

'Of course, my husband thinks it's the actor. But then he never did like him, or his wife . . .' Mrs Woolrich gave Harrison a meaningful look. 'Particularly his wife. She is not a moral woman.'

'No,' Harrison agreed. 'You could call her many things but not that.'

'I don't want you to think we're just a pair of mad old folk beating our Bibles and crying foul. The Lord gave us choice and she must live her life as she chooses. Still, my husband doesn't trust them. He never did approve of Georgina working there. But times are hard and you find the work you can get. She was a good girl, she wouldn't be so easily swayed by their charms.'

'You don't think she would have gone out with them?'

'Oh, I don't say that. Georgina was a girl and girls love glamour.' The small woman smiled. 'I'm not so old I don't remember that. An opportunity to dress up, feel special. Yes. Georgina would have gone with them. Though I can't say I understand why they wanted her to.'

Harrison said nothing, not wanting to stop her flow. He just raised an encouraging eyebrow.

'Well, now, I loved my Georgina but she wasn't from their world. For them everything's about image and importance, isn't it? It's about being seen to be the best, the richest, the most important. Would a person like that really want to be seen with their maid? God may think we're all equal but a great many of his children don't agree.'

Harrison nodded. 'It seemed out of character to me, too.'

'Georgina would tell us about them, of course. She had nothing bad to say about the husband, Frank Nayland. He was, by all accounts, a quiet and reasonable man. The wife? Not so much. She had a temper on her, that one. She certainly wasn't back - wards in letting her staff know what she thought of them. When she could be bothered to acknowledge them at all, that is. Is that the sort of woman who thinks a night out with her maid is a good idea?'

'No, Mrs Woolrich, it isn't.'

'And then there's this business of her asking to be dropped off miles away. If she was wanting to hide where she lived she would have picked somewhere a little closer to home, don't you think? She could have had him pull up outside the Balthazar Hotel. It's only six blocks away and she'd have been home in twenty minutes.'

'It doesn't make much sense, does it?'

'No, Detective, it doesn't. I was at a loss to understand how your colleague thought it did.'

'I think he was swayed by the fact that several eyewitnesses claim to have seen your daughter in the company of Mr Nayland and his wife.'

'Any of them know my Georgina? It could have been anyone.'

Harrison agreed with her again. 'You couldn't say for sure that it was your daughter in the photograph?'

For the first time, Mrs Williams looked surprised. 'Photograph?'

Surely not, Harrison thought. Even a man as lax as Grierson wouldn't have been so ham-fisted as to not show her the photograph. Depends when it came in, he realised: he'd made his decision and couldn't be bothered to make another trip out here just to show a blurry picture.

'He didn't show you?' Harrison asked, opening the small file and pulling out the image. 'A photographer took a picture of them all. To be honest with you it's a terrible shot – they're so blurred that it could be anybody.'

'Blurred or not I'd know my daughter, Detective,' she replied, taking the photograph from him.

'Yes,' he admitted, 'I suppose you would.'

'And I'm certainly not looking at her now,' announced Mrs Woolrich, offering the picture back to him.

'Are you sure? I mean . . . forgive me, I don't mean to doubt your word but this is vitally important. How can you tell that the woman in the picture isn't your daughter?'

'Because unless Mr Nayland is a lot shorter than I've been led to believe, the woman sitting next to him is a good foot too tall to be my Georgina. She would also never wear a dress like that.'

'We believe they gave the dress to her.'

'That's as maybe but she's obsessed about her bust.' Mrs Woolrich seemed slightly embarrassed by this. 'I suppose all girls are at that age. The truth of the matter is that she didn't have one. My husband caught her trying to pad out her jumper when she went out to a dance. By God, he rained terror on her that night.' She pointed at the picture again. 'The woman in that picture clearly doesn't have the same problem.'

No, Harrison conceded, looking at the blurred figure, she didn't.

So they had lied. But then he had already known that, really. The whole business hadn't made a lick of sense to him from the minute he'd first heard it. At last he had something to back up his suspicions.

'So who was it?' Mrs Woolrich asked. 'And if they didn't go out with my Georgina what became of her?'

'A good question, Mrs Woolrich. Rest assured that I will be doing my very best to find out.'

'I have nothing against the movies,' she said, as if he had asked her opinion. 'My husband says they're the work of the devil but then he says that about so many things . . . Still, I wonder what it is about those pictures that seems to dazzle everyone so. For a business that should be all about seeing it does seem to drive so many people blind.'

Back at the station that blindness seemed more profound than ever.

'So the mother says she doesn't recognise the girl,' Brunswick said, shrugging. 'She has better eyes than most. A picture like that . . . that could be my wife for all I know and she's five foot and a brunette.'

'If that was your wife,' said Grierson, still rankling at the suggestion that he had shirked his duty, 'she'd be on her knees under the table.'

'Screw you.'

Harrison ignored them. 'I'm going over there to get things straight,' he said. 'To hell with who they are.'

'At this time?' Brunswick looked at his watch. The afternoon was creeping into evening. 'They'll be pleased to see you, I'm sure, while they get ready to hit the town and keep the gossip sheets filled.'

'They'll have to make time,' Harrison insisted.

'Who's this we're talking about?' asked Flatley, a seedy little man who appropriately enough worked Vice. It was a standing joke in the depart - ment that he had found his perfect post, his shift playing out as a hobby rather than as work.

'Elizabeth Sasdy,' said Grierson, miming what he considered the actress's greatest attributes.

'Then you'll be booted off the drive before you can even show them your warrant card,' said Flatley. 'They're hosting a party there tonight and the guest list is as exclusive as hell.'

'I'm a goddamned police officer!' said Harrison. 'I don't need an invite!'

Flatley shrugged. 'Yeah? See how far that gets you when you ring the bell.'

Harrison got up from his desk, disgusted by the lot of them. A party, was it? Well then, he'd just have to crash it.

THIRD REEL: THE PARTY

THE CAMERA TAKES A SLOW PAN ACROSS THE DUSTY BRUSH-LAND OF THE HOLLYWOOD HILLS. IT'S DUSK AND THE LIGHT IS FADING QUICKLY.

Every piece of civilisation is built on another. Nothing in this world is ever empty, clean or new. A few hundred years ago this whole coast was nothing but wide-open space. A place of nature and the indigenous men and women who lived off it. A simpler land, where man and beast coexisted effectively: one ate the other, the other fought back, both sides had their share of victories and meat for their bellies.

Then the settlers came, bringing their wood and concrete, their steel and gold. Los Angeles became a city, spreading out across the coast. Then

Hollywood: first its own town, then a part of the greater whole as expansion met expansion and the ground between them was eaten away.

Up here in the hills some sign of that lost land is still to be found. The rocks are ancient, the plant life thick, and when the hot winds sweep in from the Mojave Desert the whole area comes alive, resuscitated by their hot breath.

The indigenous tribes may have gone but nature is a hardy thing and it thrives where it must. The agaves take root in shallow soil, the bougainvillea creeps its beautiful way across the walls of the new settlers who cling to these inclines so that they can look down on the world they have helped to make. In among their flowers and deep green leaves the plants' thorns grow sharp, willing to fight for space in this dwindling paradise.

The animals too still wander among the canyons. The deer forage, the coyotes prowl, feasting from garbage cans if they must. Animals are not as proud as humans – they survive however they can, grateful for each meal.

They would think nothing of the business this stretch of land has seen lately, of a woman who has fed off others in order to remain strong and beautiful. To them it would be business as usual and they would have understood her need. Indeed, a small coyote pack who have made the canyon bordering the home of Elizabeth Sasdy and Frank

Nayland their home would even feel gratitude were they capable of such emotion.

They found the body of Georgina Woolrich the very night Nayland dumped her there and they fed well. The meat was dry but it filled their stomachs and was particularly well received by the mother of the pack, her unborn pups weighing heavy inside her.

The pack left little of Georgina. Nature is not wasteful. Cracked bones and scraps of a dress as red as her meat would dry crisply in the sun of the following days.

The scent of human meat drew them closer to the buildings. One in particular, an old barn in the centre of an orange grove, called to them as they roamed their ever-widening feeding ground. There was meat here, their sensitive noses told them as much. In the darkness they scratched at the doors and stretched their snouts towards the windows. They could not get in. They wouldn't give up: tenacity rewards the hunter and this was a feast that would be worth the effort.

Just as the wild dogs gathered around the scent of Elizabeth's slaughter, the animal pack of Holly - wood drew close to her home. Tonight was a night of celebration, a party that promised to go down in history. Of course, most of the attendees affected an air of indifference: even humans understood that an animal should not show excessive weakness, that to do so was a way of offering your throat to the predator, of marking yourself out as a victim. Beneath their casual pretence the mood was high. Elizabeth's parties had once been a mainstay of the Hollywood calendar among those with the tastes to enjoy them. Talked about in knowing whispers, carnal battlegrounds where the masks of day were shed in favour of a raucous night of freedom, of submitting to the animal instincts.

Some of the regulars had grown out of their habits, age or disease having robbed them of their appetites. They were replaced with younger stars, glittering faces that had never experienced a night in Elizabeth's gardens but had certainly heard of their reputation. An indelible part of Hollywood's secret history, the font of the illicit gossip that still thrived to this day.

As night fell, cars began to gather along the driveway and the road beyond – gleaming Chryslers, La Salles and De Sotos. The natural whiff of late-summer flowers mingled with expensive scents, the after-trail of rich colognes and decadent perfumes.

Beauty had come to play.

The staff were prepared, Patience having hired extra help for the evening. Their orders were explicit and she marched in front of them before the evening began, instructing them like an army sergeant about the limits of their jurisdiction.

'You will serve the ground floor of the house and the periphery of the gardens,' she explained. 'You will keep drinks filled and the food moving. You will not, however, enter the gardens or go upstairs: both of those areas are out of bounds and anyone found breaking that rule will never find work in this city again.' Patience looked at them directly, making sure there was no doubt over this most important rule. 'Is that understood?'

'Yes, ma'am,' came the scattered response.

She fixed them with one last meaningful glare and then commanded them to their posts.

Not far away the rest of the night's staff were receiving a similar, if slightly more casual, pep talk.

Marie, installed within an ornate pagoda at the centre of the garden, wafted at herself with a highly decorated Japanese fan. Robert stood close by, as always, an implacable slab of muscle in his uniform.

'Right, my darlings,' she said. 'We all have a long night ahead of us and I need hardly remind you of the important details: there is no such word as "no" and what happens in this garden stays in this garden. This is our little paradise and we are its willing serpents. Coil and hiss for me, my loves.'

'We certainly will if the buccaneer is coming,' joked one of the girls, taking the arm of the man next to her and giggling.

'Everyone who is anyone will be here,' said

Marie, 'and need I remind you that their names are not yours to utter? Our services are sweet and invisible, our clients equally so. I don't care if you find yourself fist deep in last year's Oscar winner, I do not expect the information to be shared, discussed or mentioned once the night is done. We are priests, my lovelies.'

'We certainly spend most of our time on our knees,' agreed the Puerto Rican boy who had been so favoured by Elizabeth a few short weeks earlier.

'And offer forgiveness and a glimpse of heaven,' Marie said. 'They are blessed to receive our benedictions. Now, away with you all. Ensconce yourselves in the bushes, tails proud and to the wind.'

She turned to Robert. 'And you, my darling, need to take your position at the gate.' She grabbed at his groin with the sort of force that one uses to check the freshness of fruit. 'Though I will miss you terribly.'

He nodded and, with one final twist, Marie waved him away.

In the kitchens a select staff were chopping, straining and piping, preparing plates of the most ostentatious food that Benito Gabrizzi could imagine. He had closed his restaurant for the night, his attention transferred entirely to the line of tables that would fill the upper terrace. He had an innate distaste for this sort of catering, where image and obscurity ranked above taste but he knew his market and played to it mercilessly. The partygoers wanted food that shone, canapés that swaggered. In truth, that was easy enough – you could fill the vol-au-vents with cat food and they'd gobble them up as long as you put an obscenely expensive truffle on top. He surveyed a truly vulgar ice sculpture of the HOLLYWOODLAND sign, the base of its glistening letters surrounded by fresh fruit peeled and splayed in unlikely and unnecessary formations.

'It is silly shit,' he mumbled in his thick Italian accent and went to smoke a cigarette.

Upstairs, the party's hosts were unequal in their enthusiasm, which was only to be expected.

'I'm surprised I'm even allowed to be here,' Nayland was moaning. 'I'd have happily stayed away.'

'Nonsense,' Elizabeth replied. 'You can't miss this, it'll be the best night of the year.'

Nayland, who knew full well that it would be a night spent watching the woman he loved doting on anyone but himself, couldn't agree.

'Considering we're supposed to be separated,' he said, 'it seems ludicrous to have me parading around here in front of everyone.'

'But it's not everyone, darling, it's only the important people and they know as well as we do that public life is a fiction, nor do they care in the least what we get up to. There'll be no press here, nobody but the most important, the most influential people in the business. I can't imagine why you would want to avoid their company – after all, you'll soon be needing all the help you can get.'

'Nicely put.'

'You know what I mean. You should be out there with a smile on your face. Drink a little, but not too much. Make love to someone exciting. Enjoy yourself.'

Nayland wasn't sure he could remember the last time he had done that but he was quite sure the skill of it was lost to him.

Elizabeth turned to face him. 'How do I look?'

'Perfect as always. Maybe I should try a little myself.'

'I can't afford the supply right now. If you wanted to dabble you should have brought more livestock.'

He chose not to focus on the terminology. It would only have made him angry. Besides, he had become sickeningly hardened to the business over the last couple of weeks. It was disturbing how all it took to stomach atrocity was repetition.

'I suppose your young man is coming?' Nayland asked, deciding to be annoyed about something a little safer.

'If you mean Henry, then I believe so, yes. Fabio was bringing him.' Elizabeth began to dress, a light-blue silk confection that wafted around her like the petals of a poisonous flower. 'Do try not to hit him again. His face is far too pretty to ruin and one more punch will put your career beyond the point of salvaging.'

'I shall avoid him like the plague.'

'Probably for the best.'

Henry arrived relatively early, unfashionable perhaps but his taxi driver had matched his enthusiasm for the night ahead and brought him to the house's front gates at a speed that would have rivalled that of the Keystone Cops. It was with something approaching nervous relief that Henry stepped out onto the drive and walked the last few hundred yards. He had arranged to meet Fabio outside, the manager exercising his usual sub-paternal desire to escort him over the threshold and introduce him to all the 'players' who were there. Henry stood a short distance away from the front door and smoked a cigarette to give the man a chance to show up. He failed to do so, and, as more cars began to appear along the driveway, Henry decided to hell with introductions, he could manage just fine by himself.

As he was heading towards the entrance another man brushed past him. Henry was surprised by his appearance: a cheap suit and a hat that looked as if its job was to hide a savage haircut rather than set off a fashionable image. He was clearly not a partygoer.

Henry came up behind him as the man started to argue with Robert who was refusing him entrance.

'But I'm a police officer,' the man said, flashing his ID. 'Party or not, I demand to be allowed to see Frank Nayland and Elizabeth Sasdy.'

'I'm afraid, sir,' Robert replied, 'that my instructions are painfully clear. Unless you are invited to the gathering you don't get in. Police officer or not.'

'I could charge you with obstruction!' the man insisted. Henry realised he was taking mental notes, slightly copying the man's posture and bearing. All actors are vampires, he thought, sucking up the lives of real people for the sake of their own performances.

'Not unless you have a warrant,' Robert replied, showing no concern whatsoever. 'If you have a warrant, then, yes, I have to allow you to enter. Otherwise you're just another visitor and no visitors are allowed tonight. I suggest you come back tomorrow.'

'This is ridiculous!' the police officer sighed. 'The damn badge doesn't mean a thing to you people.'

'Is there some sort of problem?' Henry asked, thinking he should do his bit to help the doorman out a little. 'I mean, is it so urgent that it can't wait until a more civilised hour?'

The policeman turned to face him and Henry actually felt slightly intimidated by the sheer weight of insistence that the man carried. From behind he had written him off as a shabby caricature, a cypher, a supporting-cast member.

Now that he was face to face with him he realised that this man could be a lead in his own right. But this was not his movie.

'And you are?' he asked.

'Henry Toth.' *One day*, he thought, *people won't have to ask me that question. I wonder if I'll miss it?*

'Actor?'

'Yes.' To hell with the fact that he hadn't appeared in a movie yet.

The policeman shook his head in open dismissal. 'The lot of you probably deserve each other,' he said and walked away.

'Well,' said Henry, slightly put out, 'I certainly hope so.'

He looked to Robert who offered him a courteous nod. 'You are most certainly on the guest list, sir. Welcome.' He opened the door.

'Thank you.' Henry walked inside. 'I was supposed to meet my manager here but he hasn't turned up yet.'

'In my experience, sir,' said Robert, 'managers are a disorganised bunch. I'm sure he'll appear in his own good time.'

'Yeah.' Henry smiled. He rather liked this man who walked a fine line between pitch-perfect servitude and rebellion. 'Well, he better hope I haven't drunk all the cocktails by then.'

He went inside.

*

Harrison saw there was little point in his trying to browbeat the doorman. He wasn't getting in by the official way so, to hell with it, he'd have to try a more unconventional method.

He walked a short way back down the drive, in case that bastard doorman was watching. Then, when he could see that Robert was otherwise distracted by more arriving guests, he cut to the side and moved into the trees that lined the property.

Working his way to the left of the house he approached its formidable wall and followed it around to the rear. If they wouldn't let him in the front door then he would just try and find another way in. There was a service entrance but that was a hive of activity. Caterers were flitting between their vans and the house, and a man he took to be the chef was smoking a cigarette and offering frustrated curses to his staff.

Harrison kept moving. A little further along he came across a cypress tree that spread its branches close enough to the wall that he felt he might stand a chance of climbing over.

'If I tear this suit,' he mumbled to himself, 'I'll send the bastards a bill.'

He pulled himself up the first stage, clambering onto one of the thick lower branches and dragging himself higher with much grunting, grazing his palms in the process. He inched his way along towards the wall but the branch began to sag as his weight pulled it down. Leaning against the wall for support he reached up and managed to get a grip on the upper bricks. Feeling a little more secure he tried to use the spring of the branch to give him a bit of momentum. He bounced up and down on it, keeping a firm grip on the wall and then jumped when the branch was at its full height, using it as a springboard to give him the extra few inches he needed to propel himself onto the top of the wall. He crouched as low as he could, only too aware that anyone in that part of the garden would see him were they to look in his direction. He glanced down. The ground was clear on the other side, with a slight bank leading upwards. He should be able to lower himself down without breaking his neck.

Harrison swung his legs over, gripping the top of the wall as tightly as he could with his already sore hands. He lowered himself down and then let go. His feet hit the ground and twisted, sending him rolling with no dignity whatsoever down the slight incline and into a lantana bush. Pulling himself free of the branches, his skin itching from the leaves, he stood up and winced as his wrenched ankle complained. It could have been worse, he decided, testing it and deciding that it was painful but not sufficiently so to stop him walking on it. God help him if he had to clamber his way back out. Knowing his luck, he would be escorted directly out of the front door in a few minutes.

Keeping to the cover of the bushes, Harrison made his careful way towards the house, not noticing that his revolver had fallen from its holster and was now lying in the dirt beneath the lantana.

Fabio was drunk. This was far from a new sensation, of course, but as he checked his watch and realised the time he cursed the fact that his limbs wouldn't move with the speed he wished them to.

He still hadn't decided what he should do about Frank and Elizabeth but one thing he had settled on was that he couldn't let Henry get mixed up with them any further. This wasn't an entirely altruistic decision, naturally: he would have enough trouble on his hands with two clients caught up in a murder case and a third would be intolerable. Still, for all his pragmatism he did have some concern for the young lad. Henry could surely have no idea of the type of woman he was getting involved with and if Fabio didn't try and extricate him from her influence who the hell would?

At least at the party there should be enough people around to avoid a scene. He could get in there, pull Henry away and then decide from a safe distance what to do about the other two. What he had seen had been terrifying enough for him to be sure that his life would mean little if it proved to be in the way of Elizabeth's plans. He would be in danger the moment they knew he had discovered their little slaughterhouse.

Fabio changed into evening dress as quickly as his clumsy fingers would allow. Henry would arrive before him, certainly. As much as he might hope that the young man would just wait for him to turn up he was sure that Henry's enthusiasm would override his patience.

Descending in a slightly dishevelled tuxedo with a skew-whiff bow tie, Fabio rallied his driver into action.

'I'm late!' he shouted as if it were entirely the other man's fault. 'You'll have to make up the time somehow.'

Eventually he was ensconced in the back of his car and heading towards the party at speed.

'You've arrived, my darling!' announced Elizabeth on seeing Henry confused by the food.

He turned away from the plates of bright colours and shapes that wouldn't fit a human mouth and put his arms around her.

'You're looking wonderful,' he said, 'as you always so effortlessly do.'

'Oh, there's effort to it,' she said, with a smile. 'Effort like you wouldn't believe.'

Further along the terrace a jazz quartet began to play. People applauded and a small crowd made its way towards them, starting to dance beneath the candle-glow of hanging Japanese lanterns.

'Would you like to dance?' he asked.

'Oh, certainly,' she replied. 'But not here. This is not the real party.'

'You could have fooled me,' Henry laughed and gestured towards the food table and its dripping HOLLYWOODLAND sign. 'You lay this on normally?'

'We're on the periphery, darling,' Elizabeth said, taking his hand. 'This is where we come to freshen up, fill our glasses and bellies. I like to cater for other appetites, as you well know.'

She led him towards the garden.

Its walls were thick with plant life, an impenetrable jungle at the centre of this beautiful house. She steered him towards a narrow stone archway that acted as its entrance. Slipping through it, Henry found himself in a loose maze. Beyond the leaves he could hear sounds of human occupancy: laughter, cries of passion and pain. In the near distance there was the sound of splashing as someone dived into the pool.

'If I'd known I'd have brought a costume,' he said.

'We provide all you need,' Elizabeth responded, leading him to the right where, around a tight corner, he was presented with an anachronism: a set of dressing rails, hatstands and an attendant who had no need of any of them, since she was naked.

'Good evening,' she said, bowing slightly. 'Welcome to Eden. Would you like to choose your face?'

Who wouldn't? thought Henry, tearing his stare away from her body and looking instead at a short set of shelves where half-masks were arranged like plates on a dresser.

'We can't have you completely naked, after all,' said Elizabeth, starting to loosen his tie. 'We must leave you some modesty.'

He stayed her hand for a moment, struck by a sudden sense of embarrassment. 'I didn't realise . . .'

'Oh hush,' she replied, knocking his hand away and taking his tie. 'In Eden we have no need for wool and cotton. Here we wear our skins.'

She pushed the tie into his jacket pocket and then removed the coat itself.

'Perhaps you would find it easier,' Elizabeth suggested, 'if I went first.' She turned her back to him. 'If you would be so kind?'

Henry reached out to unfasten the catch at the back of her dress, his gaze moving to the attendant again, conscious that she was their audience. Her head was still slightly bowed but the soft contented smile on her face gave him some confidence. She was certainly not here to judge.

Elizabeth shed her dress, stepping out of it, a transformed creature emerging from its cocoon.

The attendant immediately moved forward,

lifted the dress from the grass and proceeded to hang it up on one of the rails.

'Thank you, my dear,' said Elizabeth, stroking her on the side of her face and kissing her on the lips. She pulled her closer, turning her head so that they were both facing Henry. 'Now it's his turn. Shall we both help him?'

She led the girl over and they set to work, alternating fingers popping shirt studs and cufflinks, rubbing across Henry's back to unfasten his cummerbund. He couldn't tell whose hand it was that manipulated the buttons on the front of his trousers but they had to work at it, his seeming shyness contradicted by the swelling they found there.

That was the point at which he let go, his erect penis helped out into the evening air. There seemed little point in remaining bashful.

The attendant dropped to her knees and began unlacing his shoes, the crown of her head bobbing against his groin as she did so.

'She's such a helpful little thing, isn't she?' said Elizabeth as Henry lifted his feet so the girl could remove his shoes. 'There's nothing she won't do to help, is there?'

The girl looked up, a serene smile on her face. 'Nothing, ma'am.'

'Who could doubt it?' Elizabeth replied, stepping behind Henry, reaching around and taking his penis in her hand. She pointed it towards the girl who took it contentedly in her mouth as if it was the most natural action in the world.

I suppose it is, thought Henry, letting go of what little inhibition he had left and pushing forward slightly.

'But we must pace ourselves,' said Elizabeth, yanking him back. 'The party hasn't even started yet.'

The attendant helped Henry shed his trousers and underwear and set about storing them on the rack as Elizabeth began to peruse the masks.

'What suits you, do you think?' she asked Henry, running her finger along their shiny enamel surfaces. They were animals for the most part, full-cheeked foxes and snarling wolves ready to growl, tear, devour.

'You choose,' he told her.

She picked up the visage of a hawk, its curled beak glinting yellow in the soft light. 'A bird of prey, I think,' she said, pushing up against him as she reached around his head to fasten it into place. 'Ready to swoop down and eat.'

'And you?'

She turned away from him and bent forward to look at the remaining masks. 'What do you think?'

Henry thought he'd missed the feel of her, stepping in behind and entering her as she gripped the side of the shelves. He looked over towards the attendant, suddenly relishing the lack of privacy. *Let her see*, he thought. *Why not?*

Elizabeth thrust backwards on to him as she lifted a mask from the shelf: a black bat, pointed ears and fangs.

'Fix me,' she said, holding it to her face so that he could tie the strings behind her head.

As soon as he had done so she pushed him back and moved away from him. Henry felt a little foolish for a moment, standing there alone. Elizabeth laughed and took his hand. 'Come on,' she said. 'I've plenty more to show you.'

Nayland felt lost within his own home. Wandering the peripheries of the garden, trying to avoid bumping into guests to whom he had no wish to speak, he looked on all around him and felt it was a place that he no longer knew. It wasn't that the trees and plants had changed, of course: it was him. The familiar surroundings now seemed to belong to another man, one who hadn't seen the things he had, done the things he had. A man of better principles and a stronger will. More than that, he felt so dislocated, so utterly broken, that he suspected there was nowhere he would now feel at home. The downward spiral was too well travelled for him to imagine ever being able to climb back up.

He sat down on the grass, listening to the sound of nearby laughter, and imagined what it might be like to kill them all. To take that final step. To finally own the blood. He pictured himself gripping Elizabeth's slaughtering knife and working his way through the cackling, hateful lot of them. He was quite sure that the world would be a better place for it. A cull of the brittle and beautiful would leave it a cleaner place. He could never do it, of course: his protagonist days were over. He was a supporting artist in this world.

A bubble of laughter erupted from the central garden and Nayland tried his hardest not to imagine what was going on in there. In the early days he had played the sex games earnestly enough but once his feelings for Elizabeth had developed he couldn't divorce his pleasure from jealousy. There was no relaxation to be found for him within the high conifer walls, just anger and resentment. There was a short-lived scream, an enthused wail of willingly endured pain and another round of laughter. He shook his head and leaned back on the grass, stretching out his limbs in an attempt to relieve them of the stressed knots they were working themselves into. The booze in him helped his head slip gently sideways as he looked up at the stars. He needed more of it – that was the only way of surviving the night.

He stood up too quickly, his drunken head spinning as blood rushed to it. Stumbling, he lost his footing on the edge of one of the planted beds and fell forward. Cursing as thorns pierced his skin and tugged at his suit, he scrabbled for purchase, hoping desperately that this latest ignoble pratfall had been private. He could imagine the gossip otherwise: 'That old drunk Frank Nayland? He's only rolling around in the flower beds like a dog . . .' He pulled himself free, planting a hand on the earth to steady himself. His hand found something unexpected, something cool and metallic. He pulled himself upright and then squatted down to investigate. It was a handgun. What the hell was a handgun doing abandoned in the bushes? Had someone hidden it there? Why? He held it up to the light, noting how much heavier it felt than the prop shooters he had carried in a number of his movies. He tried to remember the limited training he had received for his appearance in *White Light*, the gangster drama for which he had received almost universal bad notices. ('Frank Nayland should stick to dapper gents,' *Variety* had suggested, 'as he is no more convincing as a hard-nose criminal than my elderly grandmother.') He found the catch for the cylinder, swinging it open and noting that it was fully loaded with what he assumed were real bullets. The gun felt even heavier with that knowledge. Here was potential in his hand. Six lives, copper-jacketed, waiting to end. It was the closest Nayland had come to feeling power in many long years.

*

Fabio arrived at the house feeling worse and worse by the moment. The alcohol and panic had combined in him to the point where it was difficult for him not to shake as he stepped out of his car and made his way up the front steps.

'Just wait for me,' he told Teodor. 'I don't intend to be long and we'll want to get out of here quickly.'

His chauffeur nodded, closed the door behind his employer and leaned back against the wing of the car.

Fabio slowed himself down as he mounted the steps to the front door, only too aware that he might fall unless he got his balance back. He just needed to get in there, find Henry, then drag the kid out – kicking and screaming if need be. He'd worry about everything else come the morning, when his brain was his own and he could think clearly.

'Good evening, sir,' said Patience as he entered the house. 'I hope you're well.'

'I'm not,' he admitted. 'Where's Henry?'

She gave him a brief disapproving look, no doubt sensing his drunkenness and anticipating trouble. 'Henry, sir?'

'Henry Toth. Christ, woman, do you not know who's supposed to be attending?'

She took a slight intake of breath, barely bothering to hide her irritation. He'd have to think about that too in the morning – he had little time for servants who got above themselves. 'That would be the young friend of Mistress Elizabeth?'

'Not for long, I hope,' Fabio replied. 'Where is he?'

'I really couldn't say. I believe I saw him by the buffet a few minutes ago but if the mistress has taken him elsewhere . . .'

Fabio smiled at that, relishing Patience's discom - fort. 'You hate working here, don't you? A thin stick of ice surrounded by so much heat.'

'I'm sure I don't know what you mean, sir.'

'Whatever. I'll find him.'

He pushed past her and headed straight out to the patio, ignoring the few calls of greeting that came his way. He wasn't interested in playing along with the social niceties.

He surveyed the crowd, desperately hoping to recognise Henry among the laughing faces. There was no sign of him.

'Shit,' he said, nervously clenching his fists.

'That's no way to arrive at a party, darling,' laughed a woman standing next to him. 'Anyone would think you didn't want to be here!'

Fabio looked at her, drunkenly recalling her last few box-office performances and ranking her in the way that only a businessman in Hollywood could. 'Surprised they even let you in,' he replied, his words slurred. 'Or has your career tanked so low they've got you working as a waitress?'

'Well!' she shouted, clearly about to rage at him in no uncertain terms.

'Shut your face,' he said, pushing past her and heading out into the garden. 'I didn't listen to you in your last three movies and I sure as hell don't intend to now.'

Fabio ignored the eruption of shocked exclamations behind him as he headed down into the leafy paradise beyond the steps.

Henry was speechless. He had heard enough stories of Hollywood debauchery – famous names bandied around at parties and clubs with their lists of tastes and indiscretions – but he had always expected the tales to be apocryphal. Hollywood built its legends big and he was sure that the stories of sex and death he had heard were no different. Entering the central courtyard beyond the maze, he began to realise that they had barely scratched the surface.

'Hollywood is about the flesh, darling,' Elizabeth said, leading him among the sideshows and installations that surrounded them, 'and here we can celebrate that with honesty. This is where we sweat for our pleasure, where we drain ourselves dry in the name of nothing more than our own satisfaction.'

There was a good deal of satisfaction to be found. No matter the orientation or taste, everything in the garden was catered for: pleasure, pain, dominance and submission.

To Henry's left there was a row of old-fashioned pillories and stocks, the kind of thing you saw filled with captured character actors in medieval movies. The prisoners here relished their captivity. There were both men and women, chained and positioned so as to expose themselves as fully as possible. Their heads were hooded, making them anonymous, inhuman, vessels to enter or be entered by. A giggling group of partygoers gathered around them, taking it in turns to work their way up and down the line.

'I'm sure this is Douglas!' called one woman as she backed onto the inflamed groin of one of the chained men. 'I'd recognise him anywhere!' The man bucked in his bonds, thrusting against her but saying nothing as she ground back against him.

'I think you're wrong, darling,' one of her companions said, squatting down to observe the joining of flesh and occasionally help it with his eager fingers. He cupped the anonymous man's balls in his palm and laughed. 'Douglas weighs far more than this!'

'Guessing is half the fun,' announced Elizabeth, walking over to join them. 'Though it doesn't really matter.' She rested her hands on the knees of a woman who was facing upwards but curled in a foetal ball while swinging between the posts of her harness. 'They're not people, not here.' She beckoned Henry over and, moving to the woman's head, she pushed her towards him. He took his direction, positioning himself so she could push the woman against him as he entered her. 'They're like all of us,' Elizabeth continued. 'Holes to be filled.' She straddled the woman's hooded head and squeezed it between her thighs.

'We're all nameless here,' she said as the woman writhed, struggling to breathe. 'Nothing but meat and bones.'

Elizabeth stepped away and beckoned Henry to follow as they left the group to switch places.

Next there was a perverted mirror of the buffet table that Henry had stood beside earlier, though the food was not so neatly served.

'The Japanese eat like this all the time,' an elderly man announced, looking like a pompous owl with his protruding belly and his feathered mask. He took a stick of carrot and inserted it into the young woman strapped down among the plates of food.

'The Japanese will do anything,' his partner added, licking a trail of pâté from the woman's thigh. 'They're all mad.'

'Hungry?' Elizabeth asked Henry as they passed.

'Not for that,' he admitted.

There was a splash from the pool and a ripple of laughter. 'A swim, then?' she suggested.

'Maybe,' he replied, staring up at a man who had been stretched cruciform on a rack, partygoers surrounding him with thin, gleaming needles. 'That's just . . .' He couldn't find the words, though they would have been lost anyway as the man moaned when a woman reached up and slid a needle into the soft meat of his buttocks.

'It takes all sorts, darling,' Elizabeth said. 'Who are we to judge?'

'I guess.' The human pincushion writhed, glistening in the faint light of the lanterns. He was a confused map of blood trails, the heads of the needles bristling from him like crime-map markers indicating the location of murder victims.

The pool was lit only from within, a shimmering blue light that played around its edges and exposed writhing, thrusting attendants.

Henry was at a loss to tell where one body started and another stopped. The partygoers had become one in the thin strip of tiles that bordered the water. Folded in and over themselves, every part of them was at play, glistening with spittle and sweat as they dragged themselves from one partner to the next.

Elizabeth jumped over them and dived into the water. Turning onto her back she swam back from the edge, beckoning to Henry with her finger. He watched her sail backwards, her legs parting and closing, parting and closing.

He stepped among the writhing people at the edge of the water, standing in the midst of them and feeling them, oiled and eager, rub up against him. Hands reached out, inviting him to join them, clutching at his legs, fingers reaching out to his erection in the hope of claiming it for themselves. He stood there for a moment, enjoying the tease, then stepped up to the water and jumped in.

He swam to Elizabeth who was, by now, pressed back against the far side.

'Get inside me,' she insisted, mounting him and flinging her arms around his shoulders.

She pushed them back into the water, Henry struggling to keep his face above the surface as she rode him.

'The scorpion and the turtle,' she whispered to him. 'You know the story?'

He shook his head.

'The turtle is swimming along the river and the scorpion asks him to carry him from one side to the other. "But you'll sting me!" the turtle complains. "If I did that we'd both drown," the scorpion replies. "I promise I won't hurt you." So the turtle lets the scorpion climb on board.' She rubbed herself against him, the water frothing around them as he tried to stay afloat. 'Halfway across the scorpion stings the turtle. "Why did you do that?" the turtle asks as it dies. The scorpion shrugs. "I can't help it," he replies. "I'm a scorpion – it's what we do."'

Elizabeth gripped him tight, his legs fighting to reach the shallow end so that he could stand up. She pressed her mouth to his ear. 'I'm a scorpion,' she said, 'and this is what I do. Will you let me sting you?'

'Yes,' Henry replied, having finally found the pool's floor. He lifted her out of the water.

She bit his neck hard enough to draw blood and pushed away from him, swimming to the side of the pool and pulling herself out and into the midst of the bodies coupling there.

He followed, staying on his hands and knees, letting himself struggle against the tide of lovers. Lips found his, hands gripped and pulled at him as he pushed forward. He could lay no claim to who or what he was touching here in the blue-tinted shadows and he didn't care. Someone took him in their mouth and he dallied a while, before deciding that he needed Elizabeth and pushing forward.

She had circled back around him, her hands gripping his shoulders and pushing him over onto his back, the others sliding out of the way to give him room.

'I want to sting,' she said, mounting him.

She rode him for a while, both of them being jostled by those on either side. Then Henry decided he wanted a say in matters and lifted her up and over so that their positions were reversed. His patience for teasing was at an end and he pounded aggressively at her, an attack as much as an act of love. A pair of hands reached out from the mess of lovers and pinned down her arms. He heard shouts of encouragement and was aware of hands at his rear, pushing him on. In his mind all these bodies had become one, a single creature folding in on itself to explore new sensations.

When they came it was to a murmur of approval and encouraged desire. He fell back from Elizabeth and he saw the other bodies fall in to replace him, like hyenas gathering around a kill. Henry let himself fall back into the water, wanting the cool, refreshing isolation that it offered.

He kicked back from the side and watched as indistinct shapes explored the woman he had just left, knowing full well that she was only too happy to be consumed.

If Harrison hadn't hated actors before he certainly would have done by now. Keeping to the edges of the party, he had been working his way around the property, keeping an eye out for Elizabeth and Nayland. Neither of them were anywhere in sight, though it was hard to tell among the laughing, identical faces that littered the place. *Everyone looks the same*, he thought, sausages shat out of the Hollywood machine, same teeth, same hair, same jewels, same vacuous conversation. These people thought the world ended beyond the studios, a no-man's-land of dust and emptiness. How quickly they forgot once they left the real world behind and existed in this vacuum of make-up and glitter. How could he ever hope to get a truthful answer out of any of them?

He looked at the buffet table and wondered if he could risk helping himself to a plate or two – there was nothing like a glimpse of food to remind you how long it had been since you ate. He decided against it. He couldn't hope to blend in with this company – the minute the guests paid attention to his clothes he would be ousted as an intruder. Besides, he wasn't here to enjoy himself, he was here to take the hosts to one side and demand that they answered some questions. The sooner he achieved that the sooner he could get out of there.

Giving up on the outside crowds, Harrison sneaked around the back of the buffet table and made his way into the house.

Patience was beginning to suspect that her time in the employ of Elizabeth Sasdy and Frank Nayland was coming to an end. Households were little empires, especially here: they rose and fell, had their moment in the sun, then faded away to dust. For all that her employers treated her as invisible, assuming she would simply function as directed regardless of what they said and did, she was no idiot. The acrimony and violence of the last few years was one thing, she could turn a blind eye to all that, it was the bickering of children and she had no interest in it. The last few weeks had been different. First there had been the disappearance of the maid – and still, for the life of her she couldn't remember the girl's name – then the sudden transformation of Elizabeth. (And had they thought she wouldn't notice? Would simply shrug her shoulders and carry on? Of course they had . . .) Even that miracle hadn't been consistent. Elizabeth went from flaunting herself to hiding herself, as if she could pass off such a clumsy subterfuge on her housekeeper, the woman who knew her better than anyone else. Whatever Elizabeth had done, whatever treatment she had endured, it was inconsistent and unreliable. That much was now obvious. It also needed regular attention, the constant day trips proved that. Both husband and wife moved around the place weighed down with their secrets, shared looks, silence and a perpetual sense of things unsaid. It was taking its toll on Nayland. Patience had always known he was a weak man, fragile and nervous, the cracks just waiting to spread. Now there seemed to be little keeping him together but alcohol and bitterness. Yes, the household empire was crumbling, the mad empress primed to set light to it all.

Part of Patience felt relieved by that prospect. The regular employment was good, obviously, and her savings were considerable after so many years in service. Still, this was no place to be. It was a poisonous house, a dangerous house. She had a strong suspicion that the maid (Geraldine? Gemma?) had found that out for herself.

Things were crumbling. She just had to hope she could escape their collapse unscathed.

Moving through into the entrance hall, she caught sight of a man who clearly wasn't a guest. (Patience knew people and this man, in his workmanlike clothes and with his awkward body language, was not someone who should be here.) Was this another sign of the impending collapse? She decided there was only one way to find out.

'Can I help you, sir?' she asked, noting with some degree of pleasure the panic that crossed his face at being caught wandering around.

'I was looking for our hosts,' he said, pausing for a moment, clearly making a mental decision before reaching into his pocket and pulling out his wallet. 'I'm with the police and I really need to ask them some questions.'

'Tonight?' She had been right, Patience decided: here was the man who might bring the whole empire down around them.

'It is urgent,' he insisted. 'I would have waited until tomorrow otherwise.'

'I'm surprised you got past the front door,' she said, knowing full well that he hadn't. The security at these parties was second to none.

Again he paused, clearly deciding how honest he should be. 'I didn't,' he admitted. 'The guy there refused to let me in so I came over the wall.'

His honesty was so unusual – these walls rang with falsehood and deception, she could scarcely remember the last time someone had been so direct inside them – that she decided to accept him. After all, if she wanted to survive the forthcoming collapse might he not be her surest way of doing so?

'Well,' she said, 'I'm sure you have your reasons, and who am I to stand in the way of the police?'

He noted her shift of mood, gave a half-smile and nodded. 'Nice to meet someone who finally wants to help an officer out.'

'I'd always do my duty as far as that's concerned,' Patience replied. 'But it can be so difficult to know what to say, can't it? To know if one should say something? When all you have are suspicions . . .'

She wondered if she was laying it on too thick. Her natural assumption had been that she would have to convince him that she was of use, that she might be someone whose testimony would make a difference. By the look on his face, though, she could tell that he was desperate for information. Her simple presence was enough to excite him without her dropping hints.

'And you have suspicions now?' he asked.

'Things are not as they should be,' Patience said.

'There's something wrong in this house – I only wish I could put my finger on it.'

'Well, perhaps I might be able to help you do just that,' he suggested. But he had no time to go any further because that was when the screaming started.

The sensation took some time to sink in for Elizabeth, her body a riot of post-coital feelings. The first clue that something was amiss came from a woman on her right.

'My God!' the woman shrieked. 'What am I lying on?'

This was followed by people shifting all around her, their passion lost as they uncoupled and pulled themselves to their feet. The woman's disgust was mirrored by others and Elizabeth sat up, looking over her shoulder to see what it was that had turned everyone's stomach. There was nothing there. That was when it clicked, when the burning of her skin began to register and she held her hands up to her face. They were terrifying: the skin hung between the bones and the soft blue light of the pool passed faintly through the translucent flesh of her palms.

'Not now,' she whispered. 'It can't happen now.' Her voice sounded like it belonged to a grave, a cracked, brittle thing that failed to convey properly the words in her head. A death rattle.

Elizabeth got to her feet, her legs unsteady, mostly because it felt as though she had several feet of rubber sheeting draped over her. Her breasts had poured themselves down her chest and the muscles in her arms were hanging down like leathery wings. *It must match my mask*, she thought, putting her spindly fingers to the bat mask that she still wore. A monster from head to toe.

A woman screamed, rubbing at her naked skin as if desperate to wipe any trace of Elizabeth away. The action was infectious, panicked yells and roars of disgust spreading through the small crowd as they pushed away from her and made a run for the exit from the garden, all lust eradicated.

Henry pushed himself out of the pool, scanning the crowd of people, trying to spot Elizabeth and failing. She reached out to him and he backed away from her, moving into the sideshow area that they had passed through earlier.

The general panic had spread here too, though those who dallied at the stocks and the buffet could hardly know what had caused such a change in mood.

'Please!' croaked Elizabeth, moving after Henry. 'Help me, won't you?'

He backed against the buffet table, dislodging the recumbent woman who rolled through plates of finger-food before running away across the lawn, her hair streaked with guacamole.

*

Fabio entered the pleasure garden just as most of the others were leaving it. He saw Henry – naked, of course, the young fool – and behind him a creature that he would scarcely have been able to believe in had he not seen its precursor earlier. By God, though, she had degenerated even further. Elizabeth now looked less than human, like something out of a Lon Chaney picture.

'Henry!' he shouted. 'Get away from her! She's dangerous, I tell you, she's a killer!'

The young man looked towards him.

'Fabio? I don't . . . what is it?'

'It's Elizabeth, you idiot, the real Elizabeth!'

'That's not . . .' Henry said, staring at the mask the creature wore. 'That can't be you.'

'Of course it is!' she insisted. 'I'm just ill, I just need you to help me . . .'

Elizabeth stepped towards him and he tried to back away. But the table was in his way and it toppled to the ground, showering them both in crudités, cheese slices and whipped cream. A large gateau crashed to the floor between them and exploded out like the head of a suicide-by-shotgun victim.

'But you're . . .' His face contorted with disgust. 'You're horrible!'

Elizabeth couldn't bear to hear that, however much she might agree. She pulled herself towards him, her stare falling on the handle of the knife that had been used to cut the cake. She grasped its wooden handle, roaring wordlessly as she fell upon him, tearing at him with her yellow nails and a sharp steel blade.

'I'm beautiful!' she screamed. 'The most beautiful thing you'll ever see.'

Fabio made to move towards them, uncertain what to do but uncharacteristically determined not to leave Henry to his fate.

'You,' came a voice from his left and he looked up to see Nayland with a gun in his hand.

'Frank! We have to stop her!' Fabio shouted, 'You can't let her go on like this!'

'You have no idea,' Nayland replied. 'No idea at all.'

'I saw you!' Fabio said. 'I saw what she does . . . the girls . . . the blood . . .'

Nayland nodded. 'It's horrible,' he admitted, 'but it's what she needs.'

He raised the gun and calmly shot Fabio in the head.

The fat man stumbled, the look of disbelief on his face turning to one of vague irritation as his legs went out from beneath him.

Elizabeth looked up from Henry's torn features, a grotesque creature squatting on his bleeding corpse.

'Oh, Frank,' she said. 'Look at what I've become.'

She stared down at Henry, his beautiful countenance now nothing more than a ruin of open wounds.

'You'll always be beautiful,' said Frank, tapping at his temple with the still-smoking barrel of the gun. 'In here.'

She looked back down at Henry as blood from his wounds pumped into the grass. Precious blood.

'That's not enough,' she said. 'Never enough.'

Elizabeth buried herself in Henry's body, rubbing herself against him in a disgusting reflection of their recent lovemaking. She smeared herself with his blood, not knowing if it would have the effect she craved but determined enough to hope.

When she raised her head again she was a vision of red. Meat hung from the wooden nose of her bat mask. The brutal countess, the very embodiment of her namesake.

'Why is it never enough?' she asked.

Nayland shrugged. 'That's life. Now run.'

Elizabeth did as he suggested, the new blood putting a spring in her step as it worked its limited magic on her decaying bones.

Harrison arrived at the garden in time to see the creature leaping through the bushes in the distance. He reached for his revolver, only then discovering its absence.

'Shit,' he said, aware that a shot had been fired and that he had little with which to defend himself. As it was there seemed to be no need. The man with the gun – Frank Nayland, he realised, recognising him from his photo – was turning it on himself rather than picking another victim. It suddenly dawned on Harrison whose gun Nayland was holding and a shitty night took one final plunge into despair. He'd be lucky not to lose his badge after all this.

'Put the gun down, sir,' he said, trying to keep his voice calm and measured. 'There's no need for anyone else to get hurt.'

'There's always a need,' Nayland replied, though after a moment's reflection he lowered the gun. 'No point,' he said. 'I died a long time ago anyway.'

He tossed the gun to the ground and Harrison dashed forward to pick it up.

The detective looked around, taking in the two dead bodies and, bizarrely, the line of naked people chained to a set of old-fashioned pillories and stocks. As one they were thrashing, their gagged mouths choking on panicked pleas to be let loose.

'What the fuck has been going on here?' Harrison wondered aloud.

Elizabeth ran, feeling every extra burst of life that coursed through her as the blood began its work. She had no long-term plan, no idea how she was going to get out of the situation she had created for herself. None of that mattered. She was a creature of the now, an animal of instinct.

She ran through the canyon, aiming for the farm-house and her supply of blood. She would restore herself, then think of the future. Maybe she could just slip away somewhere – or maybe she could even blame it all on Nayland? After all, would anyone really believe her capable of the things she had done? Surely not. The world loved her. The world would forgive her anything. Just as soon as her beauty was returned. As soon as she was her-self again.

It took her half an hour to reach the farmhouse, her feet bleeding but beneath her attention, a ragged, wild-haired beast painted black in the moonlight with the blood of her lover, the man she had intended to marry.

To hell with him. There would be others.

Elizabeth had to force the lock on the door, using the handle of an axe that lay in the undergrowth nearby. She roared her frustration at the chain but the links were only as strong as the handles they were looped through and they couldn't keep her out for long.

Once she was inside she ran to the bathtub, fetching a heavy jar of blood and tipping it in. She climbed in, looking up at the still-swinging bodies of her donors. Two parallel beams of moonlight lit them up like spotlights on premiere night.

'Not me,' Elizabeth said, ladling the blood over her as she stared up into their dead eyes. 'Never me.'

Eventually she climbed out of the bath, dripping a trail of blood behind her as she walked towards the open doorway and into the light beyond.

She was exhausted, barely able to keep her balance as everything finally caught up with her, the adrenalin burned away in a last desperate act of self-preservation.

She would clean herself up in a moment, she decided, but it was best to make sure that the blood did its work first. Maybe that had been the problem, maybe she hadn't let it soak in for long enough?

Outside the cool air chilled her wet body. She shivered, nipples stiffening on breasts that she was once more proud to call her own. She smiled and leaned back against the door, absurdly happy, guiltless and free.

There was a growling from the darkness of the trees. It was too dark to see anything but she heard a low snort from a few feet to her left, then another from her right and, out of the night, the pack of coyotes began to advance.

It took her a moment to register that she was in real danger. She had become so accustomed to her invulnerability, so convinced that she was untouchable by anyone or anything that for an instant even the sight of these wild dogs as their snarling faces emerged into the moonlight around her seemed like something that was beneath her.

'Scat!' she shouted, kicking dust at the leader of the pack. 'Get away!'

It ignored her, growling once more and exposing its fangs as it continued to advance.

Elizabeth turned to run back inside. Her wet feet skidded in the trail of blood she had left behind her and she fell forward, hitting the ground with a cry, the door still wide open behind her.

'Stupid,' she said, holding her hand up to her mouth, lips swelling from where her face had hit the ground. 'Hit my face. Beautiful face.'

Behind her, the lead coyote gave one last growl before it jumped. Elizabeth rolled over, desperately trying to hold it off with her hands. It was far too strong, and it was not alone as the rest of the pack descended, wild with hunger at the scent of blood and old meat, drooling from their jaws at finally being let in here to the building that had called to them for so long.

'Not my face!' Elizabeth screamed as the beast's jaws snapped a mere inch from her nose. 'Not my beautiful face!'

The coyote snapped at her fingers, tearing them away at the knuckles before lowering itself to her throat. It clamped down with its jaws and yanked them up. Elizabeth gave one last gurgling shriek.

The coyote agreed with her on one point: her face *was* beautiful. The closest that a coyote could come to such an appreciation flashed through its animal mind as it tugged at the flap of flesh below her chin and tore it from her still-screaming skull. Rich and wet, it slipped down the creature's throat like a blood-soaked caul. It was very beautiful indeed.

NEWSPAPER HEADLINES APPEAR ON-SCREEN:
'HUNGARIAN ACTRESS ON THE RUN AFTER KILLING MAID'
'"SHE KILLED FOR BLOOD!" CLAIM POLICE OFFICERS IN SASDY INVESTIGATION.'
'COUNTESS DRACULA! – THE HOLLYWOOD HORROR CONTINUES!'
'"SHE MADE ME HELP HER," INSISTS FRANK NAYLAND. "I TRIED TO STOP HER . . ."'

[INTERTITLE: THREE WEEKS LATER]

THE CAMERA PASSES THROUGH THE BARS OF A POLICE CELL TO FIND NAYLAND, A BROKEN MAN, BEARDED AND PALE, A SHADOW OF HIS FORMER SELF, LYING ON A BED. DETECTIVE SCOTT HARRISON ENTERS, GIVES NAYLAND A LOOK OF OPEN

DISGUST, THEN SITS DOWN ON A CHAIR THAT HAS BEEN BROUGHT IN FOR HIM.

'Looks like you're going to get away with it,' said Harrison, not hiding the contempt in his voice.

'A probable life sentence? For helping her hide a body?' replied Nayland. 'Hardly getting away with it.'

'You shot a man.'

'Only by accident – how many times do I have to tell you? Elizabeth was killing that poor boy and I was trying to save him.'

'But you missed and shot your manager smack in the head. Yeah . . .'

'You still don't believe me?'

'Of course I don't. It's bullshit and any sensible jury would smell it a mile off.'

Nayland fixed him with a blank stare. 'We'll see. You may get the climax you want after all.'

Harrison shook his head. 'Nah . . . they'll let you get away with it because you're you. You're the man they know from the silver screen, the hero, the man they think they know just because they've paid a few dollars to see you over the years.'

'All I ever did was try to entertain.'

'No. You're a professional liar and as far as I'm concerned you've never stopped.'

Nayland shrugged and looked away. 'Believe what you like.'

Harrison got up and walked out, unable to spend a moment longer with the man.

Outside, finally able to breathe fresh air, he unclenched his fists and leaned against his car, trying to get his anger under control. The man was guilty, guilty of far more than being a lousy shot and a weak-willed idiot who helped to cover up a murder committed by his wife. But there was no way he was going to be able to prove as much so what choice did he have but to let it go?

He looked up to see a billboard looming over him. It was advertising a new movie, *Crime Without Passion*.

'No such thing,' he told it. Then he got in his car and drove away.

CODA

'You're shitting me!' laughed Tony Riggers. 'You're telling me he got away with it? Your story needs work, my friend.'

He walked off, laughing and shaking his head. Leo stared at the old man, still standing in front of the broken patio doors, half silhouetted against the bright sky beyond.

'It does seem a bit far-fetched,' Leo said, feeling that he ought to offer some opinion as he was still, at least nominally, the man in charge here.

'I liked it!' said Cheryl, holding her friend's arm tight, kids sitting beside the campfire listening to scary stories.

'Well, I thought it was disgusting,' announced Margaret Riggers, 'and certainly not the sort of thing I paid my money to listen to. You can rest assured that I will be asking for a refund.'

Good luck with that, thought Leo but said nothing as she marched back outside to join her husband.

'I can't help the facts,' the old man said. 'They are what they are.'

'Hang on, though,' said Vonda. 'So you're saying the police only ever found out about Georgina, the maid? All the other women they killed, all those prostitutes, that went undiscovered?'

Holdaway nodded. 'They had no reason to look into it any further, did they? They'd never have believed that the blood had that effect on Elizabeth. The people at the party didn't want to come forward and offer evidence of what she looked like at the end – they hid away and kept their secrets, just like Hollywood always does. The only other man who knew their secret was Fabio and he was dead. All the police had to go on was a missing maid and the dead bodies at the party.'

'OK,' Leo said. 'I get that, but it still doesn't make sense. As you say, there's only three people who knew about it so . . . how come you do?'

Holdaway smiled at that and reached into his jacket pocket. 'Because my name's not really Gary Holdaway,' he admitted, pulling out a small handgun. 'It's Frank Nayland – and you're all going to help me make a comeback.'

IMAGE: A NEWS CLIP SHOWING THE HANDSOME FACE OF A YOUNG MAN WAVING AT THE PREMIERE CROWDS.

THE TEXT READS:

Rising star and winner of the *Variety* 'One to Watch' award this year, Gary Holdaway, wowed audiences last night at the premiere of his new star vehicle *Shatterstar*. 'I'm just so glad to be given this opportunity,' he told our reporter. 'You have no idea how long I've dreamed of this moment.'

FADE TO BLACK

Hands of the Ripper
Guy Adams

A new novelisation of the classic Hammer film

He is raising the poker again and Anna bites her lower lip so hard she chokes a little in the blood that runs down her throat . . .

On a cold, wet night recently widowed psychology lecturer John Pritchard visits spiritualist Aida Golding with his son. Although wary, something has driven him here. And he is drawn to a troubled young woman who is trying to contact her child. Something about her intrigues him and despite his doubts he continues to attend meetings.

One night at an intimate séance in Aida's house the lights go out and one of the group is brutally murdered. John has his suspicions but he can't prove anything. He senses that Aida has some hold over the girl and he offers her a place of refuge in his home. But the past haunts Anna in the most chilling of ways. And all too soon John realises he's made a terrible mistake.

HAMMER

AN EXCLUSIVE MEDIA COMPANY

About Hammer

Hammer has been synonymous with legendary British horror films for over half a century. With iconic characters ranging from Quatermass and Van Helsing to Frankenstein and Dracula, Hammer's productions have been terrifying and thrilling audiences worldwide for generations. And with the forthcoming film, *The Quiet Ones*, there is more to come.

Hammer's literary legacy is now being revived through its new Partnership with Arrow Books. This series will feature original novellas which will span the literary and the mass market, the esoteric and the commercial, by some of today's most celebrated authors, as well as classic stories from more than five decades of production.

Hammer is back, and its new incarnation is the home of cool, stylish and provocative stories which aim to push audiences out of their comfort zones.

For more information on Hammer,
including details of official merchandise, visit:
www.hammerfilms.com

AN EXCLUSIVE MEDIA COMPANY